Praise for the Night Stalkers series:

"Top 10 Romance of 2012."
– Booklist, *The Night Is Mine*

"Top 5 Romance of 2012."
–NPR, *I Own the Dawn*

"Suzanne Brockmann fans will love this."
–Booklist, *Wait Until Drk*

"Best 5 Romance of 2013."
–Barnes & Noble, *Take Over at Midnight*

"Nominee for Reviewer's Choice Award for Best Romantic Suspense of 2014."
–RT Book Reviews, *Light Up the Night*

"Score 5 – Reviewer Top Pick – Buchman writes with unusual sensitivity and delicacy for such a hard-edged genre."
–Publishers Weekly, *Bring On the Dusk*

The Night Stalkers 5E

Target Lock on Love

by

M. L. Buchman

Published by Buchman Bookworks

Discover more by this author at:
www.mlbuchman.com

Cover images:
Helicopter on the valley at sunset
© Fotolotti | Dreamstime.com
Young happy couple together on sandy beach embracing outdoors © Olga Reutska | Dreamstime.com
Dog Tags Four © Lightpainter | Dreamstime.com

Other works by this author:

The Night Stalkers
The Night Is Mine
I Own the Dawn
Daniel's Christmas
Wait Until Dark
Frank's Independence Day
Peter's Christmas
Take Over at Midnight
Light Up the Night
Christmas at Steel Beach
Bring On the Dusk
Target of the Heart
Target Lock on Love

Firehawks
Pure Heat
Wildfire at Dawn
Full Blaze
Wildfire at Larch Creek
Wildfire on the Skagit
Hot Point

Delta Force
Target Engaged

Angelo's Hearth
Where Dreams are Born
Where Dreams Reside
Maria's Christmas Table
Where Dreams Unfold
Where Dreams Are Written

Dieties Anonymous
Cookbook from Hell: Reheated
Saviors 101

Thrillers
Swap Out!
One Chef!
Two Chef!

SF/F Titles
Nara
Monk's Maze

Chapter 1

As the Little Bird helicopter bucked its way through the early October storm, Lieutenant Mick "The Mighty Dozer" Quinn wasn't too worried; it wasn't that much of a storm. Especially not by Gulf of Alaska standards. But it did think that slapping their helicopter, the *Linda,* about the sky was good sport and that was making him work for it.

Thirty, twenty, and two.

Thirty-knot winds—thirty-five miles-an-hour to landlubbers. Twenty-foot waves—not even enough to slow down his family's commercial crabbing operation. And two miles visibility—if it hadn't been the middle of the night.

The storm they were flying into would soon cut that to thirty, twenty, and a hundred yards. As usual, the Aleutian Islands were wrapped in crappy weather and ice cold water that always found a way down the back of your neck. He didn't miss that, but he still missed working on the family boat sometimes.

"This is nuts! Like way worse than even cashews." The storm was, however, pissing off his copilot. Ready to take on Mother

Nature womano-a-womano, Patty O'Donoghue snarled at her opponent through the windscreen. Patty was always on the attack and she'd be immensely irritating if she wasn't so funny about it. And so damned competent.

"It's—squall line in a hundred yards—doing this just to spite us," she fed him critical information slipstreamed right in with her grousing.

They worked closely together, very closely. Their AH-6M attack helicopter was the smallest manned rotorcraft in the US military's arsenal. It fit just two people, and it was a good thing that Patty wasn't as wide shouldered as he was or they'd be crammed in the tiny helo's side-by-side seats. Though she wasn't a slip of a thing either; just right, he supposed, for a sassy, kick-butts-now-and-take-names-later soldier.

The rear seat could have held two more people. Except the *Linda* was the attack version of the Little Bird—which was why he'd named her for Linda Hamilton in *Terminator II.* The back seat had been replaced by large ammunition cans with feed belts running out to the guns mounted to either side of the fuselage. Just like Sarah Connor, their helicopter was trim and dangerous as all hell.

"It isn't nuts. I used to work on the Alaskan crab boats," Mick nodded down at the roiling sea just fifty feet below them. "My family's probably out there working right now."

"Big whoop, Quinn. I worked the boats on the Grand Banks outta Gloucester." Then she laughed, "No wonder"—it came out *one-de;* her accent always cracked him up—"we went Ah-mee. Still say this hee-ah mission is nuts." The accent that JFK imitators had turned into a national joke was apparently still alive and well in Patty's corner of the country.

The reasons he'd gone Army had nothing to do with the sea. Or maybe everything to do with the sea, but not in the way Patty meant.

"I mean seriously nuts," she waved a hand at the rain-swept darkness ahead then cycled back through checking all of the helo's systems. "Five percent falloff in power due to the damp air. Compensating fuel flow."

"*Damp* air?" They had just plunged into the leading edge of the storm with a sharp slap. Rain now pounded against their windscreen as they hustled along at a hundred and fifty miles an hour. The wind and engine noise vied for which could be louder.

"Barely worth pulling on a sou'wester for, Quinn."

"This mission is no nuttier than you, Boston." Much to his copilot's irritation, their commander's nicknames stuck and stuck hard. When Major Pete Napier tagged you, it stuck, even harder than those of his second-in-command, Captain Danielle Delacroix. Danielle's previous tag for her had been "Irish Patty" but Napier had changed that to "Boston" and all of Patty's protests that she was from Gloucester were dismissed out of hand. Mick saw no reason to ease up on her just because they'd flown together for two years of training and the three months since.

He hadn't minded Danielle tagging him as "The Mighty Quinn" from Bob Dylan's song *Quinn the Eskimo.* He wasn't an Alaska Native, though his family had been up there since the gold rush days. Great-Gran was rumored to have taken an Alutiiq lover at one point—in portraits, his grandma certainly hadn't fit in with her older sisters. Then it had skipped a generation and he liked that he favored Gran; she'd certainly been a tough old bird—still was for that matter even if she didn't ride the crab boats anymore.

Major Napier had taken one look at his broad fisherman's shoulders and tagged him as "Dozer." Danielle had blended the two to Mick "The Mighty Dozer" Quinn.

Didn't matter, he answered to any of them. But Patty couldn't just shrug it off; she really cared about such things.

He stayed focused on flying them through the storm without accidentally flying into the ocean. That's what he cared about, deeply—pun intended, they were now passing over the deep Aleutian Basin. Not that it really mattered. If he made a mistake, it would be the top ten feet of ocean that would kill them, not the ten thousand below that.

Tonight was a typical Night Stalkers' mission, at least for the 5th Battalion E Company. No one could quite agree on what the "E" stood for—other than coming next after the D Company—but "Extreme" was a popular candidate. Tonight's mission was definitely a walk on the wild side: take your four helicopters, fly out into utterly disgusting conditions, mess with the enemy's head, don't get caught.

And so here they were; four in formation, flying west over the Aleutian Island chain in the dead of night.

He flew his Little Bird *Linda* close beside the Black Hawk *Beatrix*. M&M and Kenny flew the 5E's other Little Bird Leeloo on *Beatrix's* opposite side. Trailing a mile behind was the workhorse of the outfit, the *Carrie-Anne*. The heavy-lifter Chinook helicopter flown by Napier and Danielle was the key to tonight's operation. The rest of them were distraction and protection. Three attack helos and one massive transport bird. It had certainly been working for them in the three months since they'd been formed up as a company.

Mick admitted it was a little unusual to be taking on the most paranoid Navy on the planet, the North Koreans. But…

"It doesn't feel atypically extreme," he teased Patty.

He could sense her shrug through their shared flight controls. The collective in his left hand beside the seat didn't lift, but he could feel the vibration of her gesture. The cyclic joystick that arced up between their knees didn't even wiggle that much. A pilot learned to isolate gestures from the flight controls.

Mick was damn glad to have Patty riding second on the controls. Flying in tandem like this helped prevent some subtle control mistake that might kill them both. A pilot as good as Patty added another layer of security, particularly in such foul conditions. He always flew at his best with her. Not that he was trying to impress her or anything, she just brought out the best pilot in him.

Along with the rain, the wind picked up another ten knots and the waves another dozen feet. He climbed to stay fifty feet above the crests.

This whole mess had started with the Chinese People's Liberation Army Navy. The PLAN had buddied up with Russia for a massive naval exercise close enough to Japan to give the Japanese a major case of hives. Then, instead of turning for home like good little destroyers and landing craft, they'd driven for US territorial waters. The PLAN didn't push three thousand miles from their home waters just by chance.

"Right of Innocent Passage, my ass," Patty grumbled.

"Kind of my thought as well, but it is the law."

Major Napier's briefing for the flight had reminded them that "innocent passage" was allowed under the UN Convention of the Law of the Sea. As long as they did nothing aggressive, like launching planes or attack watercraft, they could sail right through another nation's territorial waters and say, "Oh, I'm not really here; just in transit."

The fact that the Chinese freaked every time the US came within two-hundred miles of their coast hadn't stopped the Chinese from steaming a loop within a five miles Attu—the farthest west of the Aleutian Islands, uninhabited since 2011. The Pentagon had displayed far more restraint than the Chinese Coast Guard by sensibly doing absolutely nothing.

Then badly misreading the situation—and unaware of the numerous tiny retributions that the Chinese were bound to suffer for a long time to come—the North Korean leader had decided that if the Chinese could flaunt the Americans, so could he.

He'd mobilized every ship that was in good enough repair to risk such a long voyage—all three of them. North Korea's navy was called a "brown water navy" with reason. Most of their vessels weren't even capable of circling from one coast of North Korea, around South Korea, and to the other side—a journey of less than a thousand miles.

Striking for the Aleutians *was* nuts, even if he'd never admit his agreement with Patty just on principal.

The first time, the Pentagon had again turned a blind eye just as they had with the Chinese. The second time the US had sent a pair of jets to do a low-level flyby that hadn't deterred the North Koreans. The third North Korean incursion had passed right between Kanaga and Tanaga Islands in the outer Aleutians—a strait less than five miles wide—to thumb their noses at the Americans.

This time, working their way up the island chain to see just how far they could push it, they had crossed past Dutch Harbor and Unalaska Island within plain sight of the Alaska ferry and innumerable fisherman. Dutch was the largest fishery port in the US and that was too much for the Pentagon. And apparently for Patty O'Donoghue as well.

"The fourth goddamn passage in four weeks is—"

"Is why we're here tonight," he cut off her rant before she could get her Irish up. Because when Patty did, she wasn't a firecracker, she was a battering ram. She made most of the other pilots psychotic after a single hour aloft.

Her sharp humor and passionate emotions worked for him, at least in flight. Whoever she finally latched onto in the personal side of her life would need the patience of Job or to be just as feisty as she was; he'd wager on the latter, with battles royal ensuing into the foreseeable future with both sides enjoying themselves immensely.

At the moment her sights were aimed at Julian, the copilot on the DAP Hawk *Beatrix*—except she hadn't taken any action yet, at least none that he'd spotted. Maybe he'd misread it. At the end of training it had been a mechanic back at Fort Campbell. Before that was a Specialist in the 101st Airborne and then...

Patty O'Donoghue was a looker with her thick, ember-dark red hair and cream skin, and could have her pick. But, man, the woman was a handful. He wished "whoever" all the luck in the world; they were going to need it.

His idea of an ideal woman was—

"Contact with Korean People's Navy group, it is in thirty miles," Lieutenant Sofia Gracie's voice whispered over the encrypted radio, rich with mellifluous tones of her Brazilian childhood and Los Angeles upbringing. "Correct bearing to three-oh-five."

He could listen to her voice all—

"You gonna fly this thing *o-ah* shall I, dream boy?" Patty interrupted his thoughts.

"Sure, Patty. Like I'd trust you at the controls." Which he did—absolutely—or he wouldn't be flying with her. She was damned good and only flew copilot because he was a little better at the flying and she was a little better at handling the weapons while he flew. He was also Lieutenant to her Chief Warrant 3 for what little respect Patty deemed that to be worth. It earned him the occasional salute, a moderately frequent "sir"—though that was often ironic—and what he felt was more than his fair share of sass.

No big deal anyway. Mick wasn't more than a second or two late in correcting his flight path to match the other three birds in the flight, all now heading directly toward the tiny KPN fleet. It wasn't like they were flying a tight formation in this weather. His primary worry was not eating a rogue wave at this low flight level.

"They don't even own a destroyer to send," Patty protested as if the KPN's finest had been sent as a personal insult to one Chief Warrant O'Donoghue. "Their only full frigate has never been seaworthy. They gotta send us *light* frigates, corvettes really. These boys really need to be spanked and sent back home."

"Which is why we're here," though he didn't waste his effort on saying it aloud. Patty was perfectly capable of sustaining the conversation on her own. Gods but the woman cracked him up.

A straight-in approach was safe enough, because the entire 5E flew stealth-modified aircraft. At fifty feet up in a storm, the Koreans' radar wouldn't see a thing of their four helicopters. Of course, if it weren't for the lovely Sofia flying her Avenger drone fifty thousand feet above them, they wouldn't be seeing a thing either.

# # #

Patty could see exactly where Mick's attention had gone; like he stood a chance. He'd been smitten since the first moment Second Lieutenant Sofia Gracie had been added to their team. All of the guys had been gobsmacked because Sofia really was that stunning. Most of them had recovered with time, but Mick wasn't one of them.

Being strictly impartial about it, Mick was a handsome enough bastard in a dark, brooding way. Black hair flowed to his collar, matching his dark eyes. It was that deep, soft voice of his that slayed Patty, though she wasn't complaining about his fisherman's physique or the way his big hands were so light on the Little Bird's controls either.

The Mighty Quinn was a solid anchor in any situation. He was always so calm and steady, no matter what storm she tossed in his direction to best him.

He was also one of the few that could keep up with her, male or female. No insult to Kenny and M&M in the *Leeloo,* but they just didn't have the feel for the sprightliness of the Little Bird helos the way that Mick did with the *Linda.* Each time she'd flown with them, they'd learned far more from her than she from them. Mick could just as easily be "Magic Man" as "The Mighty Quinn" for what he could make their aircraft do.

Not that she'd ever consider telling him. If his head ever became as swollen as his shoulders, she'd have to copilot from the outside of the helicopter rather than the left-hand seat. The stealth aircraft flew with its doors on, unlike most Little Birds—the door had a lower radar signature than a pilot sitting in their seat. Mick was an easy man to share the cramped space with.

But if he thought all that was enough to win him "Latin Lady's" undying affection, then good luck to him. Patty hadn't seen Sofia pick up even a single hint, not that Mick had dropped one either. Dumb. Guys were so damn dumb.

Sofia was in some whole other class of woman that was way above a guy who was merely dark and handsome. She should be modeling women's underwear or doing Miss Clairol commercials with that swirling dark hair and her Brazilian-brown skin. Or Estée Lauder with those dark, dark eyes.

But she didn't.

She was an awesome Avenger pilot. Of course that meant that she and her copilot flew their remotely-piloted aircraft from a cargo container packed with high-tech gear currently parked at Joint Base Elmendorf-Richardson—typically called a "coffin" for its long, low shape. JBER was eight hundred miles away back in Anchorage, but satellite communications made that irrelevant. No matter that she wasn't physically present, because she did it damn well. She had proved several times that she knew exactly what to do with her drone—sorry Sofia—her jet-powered RPA that flew ten miles up at four-hundred-and-fifty miles-an-hour.

Sofia was also an easy person to like. Maybe there was some way Patty could encourage Mick, but sabotage him with Sofia at the same time just for the hell of it. Nah! The few times she'd stuck her foot in someone else's mess, she'd only made it worse… and then gotten caught. Didn't matter; she had faith that the big lummox would find a way to fail all on his own. Too bad; they'd look good together. Of course, any man would with Sofia on their arm.

And now it was time to look good for the North Koreans... who would never see them coming.

Fifty feet up, they should pick up the Korean's top-of-mast radar at ten miles out.

"Five. Four. Three. Two…" She stretched it out, but shouldn't have. Right on cue, the KPN's radar sweeps blasted onto the Little Bird's passive detection systems.

"How do you do things like that?"

"*Shit* like that, Quinn. For God's sake, loosen up. And it's because I'm that goddamn good. Not that it matters. Look at the frequency these guys are using," she waved at hand at the console, knowing Mick didn't have time to look down. "They're running tech that the Army retired back while you and I were still pooping up our diapers, or at least you were. I was always a dainty little child."

"Uh-huh," Mick's grunt might have been long-suffering or it might have been a tease. Man's grunts were hard to read.

"The KPN's radar uses such a broad sweep that we could fly right between their lines of resolution. Even Danielle's big-ass Chinook could do that."

Why was it that the ever so classy Danielle flew the monstrous, twin-rotor *Carrie-Anne?* Of course flying in a Chinook MH-47G named for the actress who played Trinity in *The Matrix*—the ultimate leather-clad kick-ass heroine—had its points.

Still, Patty could have enjoyed flying her Little Bird with Danielle, not that she wanted to trade Mick even one little bit. Not only was he exceptional as a flier, but if your pilot was supposed to be eye candy, Mick fit that bill very nicely too.

But Danielle had so much smooth sophistication that Patty knew she totally lacked. If they flew as a girl-girl team, it would have been fun…and maybe a little of the effortless elegance would have rubbed off on her.

"Too bad for the KPN," Mick didn't sound sorry at all, "that we're stealth rigged. All that energy spent looking for something they'll never see."

"Poor bastards," Patty agreed. The storm was beating on them now, thick with rain and hard winds. The KPN's ships were all in the two- to three-hundred foot range, but narrow enough that they rolled hard in the rough waves. Even for people she didn't like, they were not having a good day…and the Night Stalkers were about to make it even worse.

"Just makes it more fun," Mick commented.

"You *are* evil and twisted. There's hope for you yet, Quinn," she grinned behind the lowered visor of her helmet which was glowing on the inside with layers of rapidly shifting tactical information.

Mick didn't let his snide out very often, but she always appreciated it when he did.

"Knew there was a reason I liked flying with you." Because whatever else The Mighty Quinn might be, he was a kick-ass pilot and a hell of a partner.

She was never as good beside any other pilot; his skill demanded her best performance be even better. *Be all you can be.* Hell with joining the Army, she'd already done that. Earn the right to fly beside Mick Quinn, that took some serious doing.

"Our target will be the westernmost ship," she filled him in. "It's also the biggest, a Nampo class. Twin 30mm machine guns, so don't mess with that. And intel says an RBU-1200—that's a five-missile anti-submarine weapon so we should be fine as long as you don't dump us in the soup."

"Wasn't planning on it," Mick stated it as if he was discussing a change in a battle plan. She really needed to find a way to loosen him up.

"They also have a helo platform, not that they have the skills to launch in this weather. Rumor has it that they're still flying Russian Mi-4 Hounds. You know those things are half a century old. It would be really cool to see one, even parked on a crap frigate. North Korea is the last nation trying to fly them."

"One minute," Major Napier, their company commander, called over the encrypted radio channel from the trailing Chinook *Carrie-Anne*. "Keep them busy."

"Dance!" Danielle called before Napier clicked off.

That was another reason to want to be like Captain Danielle Dellacroix.

Dance.

It was one of those crazy commands that the captain had cooked up during training—back before they'd been formed into the 5E and Pete "The Rapier" Napier took command.

If Patty could be any other woman, it wouldn't be the curvaceous Sofia Gracie; it would be Captain Delacroix with her soft-spoken Québécois French accent and exceptionally strategic mind. Though if she'd been Danielle, she'd now be married to Major Pete Napier and Patty would have killed his ass in the first month. He'd be damned irritating if he wasn't such a good commander.

So, not Danielle.

Patty would find her boy someday. But he wouldn't be a fisherman, who thought a pretty woman on a working boat was an open invitation. The first real attack had only been averted because she happened to be in the galley and could grab a knife. After that, she'd learned to always have a blade handy and still had to flash it at the occasional overeager asshole to convince them that "No!" meant no. Two of them she'd had to scar but good before they'd backed off.

And it wouldn't be some gung-ho Army pilot too damn sure of himself. If she never heard some airjock say "Come fly me!" then ask if she still had her stewardess uniform again, it would be too soon. She'd had enough of those kind of creeps who didn't like the fact that she could out fly every one of their asses. By that time she didn't need a knife, the Army had trained her plenty well in hand-to-hand combat. Switching to Special Operations had only honed those skills.

She glanced over at Mick. And it sure as hell wouldn't be someone who was both fisher and pilot no matter how handsome.

In the meantime she had every intention of enjoying herself. She'd taken up with teasing Julian over on the *Beatrix*. But it was just to mess with his head, there was nothing ever going to happen there. As it was, she'd been having a long dry spell and was just fine with that.

Dance, Danielle had said. She'd just instructed each of the pilots to implement evasive tactics based on their favorite music. Better than something *Star Trekish* like "Execute Evasion Plan Delta." The military's top pilots would each dance differently and it made the flight wholly unpredictable and nearly impossible to target. It also meant…

"Oh, man! You are *not* gonna hit me with country," she aimed her complaint at Mick over the on-board intercom. She checked that all weapons' systems were armed and ready in case the North Koreans were dumb enough to actually try and engage American aircraft while sailing in American waters.

"Only the finest," Mick began humming some Tim McGraw song.

"Goddamn it, Quinn. How is it possible that a perfectly respectable girl knows that's a Tim McGraw song? You're ruining me."

"Because a perfectly respectable girl *would* know it was Tim McGraw."

"That's not true!" Patty resisted the urge to stomp a little rock and roll into the rudder pedals as he began making the Little Bird shift and sway.

"It is," Mick continued placidly. "Which begs the question of how you know anything about it."

So much worse than that, she even knew the words well enough to sing along—which she absolutely wasn't about to do. "I'm gonna request a goddamn new pilot; one who knows decent music when he hears it."

He hummed even louder over the intercom until it was resonating inside her helmet.

"Keep it up and you're gonna be so dead that you'll be way past living like you still had any dying to do."

Patty knew it was a mistake as soon as she said it.

Mick broke into full song with the last line of the refrain, which is what she'd just done her best to mangle. Then he began all over going on all about skydiving and climbing mountains—the helicopter swooping and slipping through the air in perfect time to his music. He wielded a good, deep baritone designed to turn a girl into a liquid puddle.

Well not her.

She fought back with Marianas Trench's *Fallout,* but she couldn't carry a tune for crap so her attempt at punk/emo didn't cut him down even a little.

At that moment, the tall sides of the frigate came into view just a dozen rotor diameters ahead. Which on a Little Bird, with its tiny five-blade, twenty-seven-foot diameter main rotor, wasn't very far.

The ship's high bow was climbing clear of a big wave and then crashing down into the next trough; a very uncomfortable-looking ride. They'd be better off in a fishing boat that could just ride over one wave at a time without all of the bucking and yawing. Military ships were built narrow to move fast, but that meant they totally sucked during a storm.

Mick hit the KPN with the song's line about riding a rodeo bull just to emphasize the point—wasn't right that a country boy could make her laugh so easily—and then he dodged aside as the frigate's forward anti-submarine rocket launcher tried to spear them when the ship took another painful roll.

The ship only had running lights on: red and green to the sides, a white all-around at the top of the mast, a second white below that pointing forward. The deck itself was ink-and-storm dark.

The North Koreans didn't notice that they'd acquired a pitch-black Little Bird helicopter hovering above their fore-deck. Of course the *Linda* was a stealth craft with its running lights out.

Mick slipped up until the Little Bird was hovering directly in front of the command bridge's windows.

"Are you feeling ignored, madam?" Mick asked Patty in an über-polite voice as if they were at some snooty Boston social event rather than a couple of fishers-turned-pilots now hovering over a ship's deck in the middle of the Aleutians.

"Why yes, good sir. I feel as if they aren't paying any frickin' attention to us at all." She raised a pinkie finger from the cyclic control, not that Mick would be able to see it.

Quinn switched to singing the Trace Adkins song about a lonely heart who turned on every light in the house to show his departed lover the way back home. Oh, what the hell! She could take a hint. So, she joined on the chorus and hit the landing light, aiming it directly into the command bridge windows.

The reaction was galvanic. It was easy to see the several seasick officers leaning against any support—brown water navy indeed. Two seamen, looking far more stoic than their superiors, clung to the wheel.

And every one of them too frozen with surprise to even cover their eyes. Korean deer staring into the headlights.

Perfect.

Because tonight's mission was to make sure that the KPN never looked astern to see what the SEAL team delivered by the Chinook *Carrie-Anne* was doing back there.

# # #

Mick watched for the first one to unfreeze; a junior officer twitched like he'd had his butt pinched.

Mick dodged the *Linda* back into the storm with all the agility of her *Terminator II* namesake the moment before the deck lights flashed on.

"Camera." It was their first really close look at a Nampo-class light frigate; though he had no time to look himself.

"Never stopped recording," Patty answered back.

"Good girl," not that he'd expected less.

"Woman!" She sniped back just as he'd planned.

"Where?"

Her growl was music to his ears.

This time he approached from the starboard side, flew directly over the bridge and disappeared to port.

"*Woman*! Like the one who's gonna shove you out on the next fly-by. Then you'll be shipped off to North Korea and no longer chapping my ass."

"So scared. Eek," he delivered it deadpan.

She spared a moment to punch him in the arm, lightly, so that she didn't jostle his control.

Mick focused on keeping the bridge crew distracted. They didn't begin to understand the high technology of his Little Bird. Across the inside of his helmet was displayed the image of any direction he looked. With a thumb control he could look up, down, even straight behind him as if he was sitting alone in the night sky without a helicopter wrapped around him. Outside, multiple mounted cameras routed thermal-enhanced seamless images onto his visor.

A slap of wind tried to slew him into the high bow of the frigate. He lifted enough to clear the railing, but kept his landing light aimed directly in their faces as the ship slewed across beneath him. Between the wind and the waves and the crap visibility, this was getting nasty even by Night Stalker standards.

"How are the others doing?" he asked Patty.

"You just focus on keeping us alive and this crew distracted."

"Spoilsport."

"Am not. I'm a woman. I get," and she went for song, "R.E.S.P.E.C.—"

"First ship tampered," Sofia reported over the radio, cutting off Patty's grossly off-key efforts. "The *Leeloo,* she is clear."

Sofia's naturally musical tones only emphasized the degree of murder that O'Donoghue had been perpetrating on Aretha.

"The wet team, it is headed now to *Beatrix's* target."

Mick was damn glad to not be on the wet team. It was a given that SEALs were comfortable in water, but this storm was ugly even from the air. From the small rubber boat that the *Carrie-Anne* had delivered astern of the KPN's ships, it must be pure hell.

Beatrix's ship was second. The Direct Action Penetrator Black Hawk was named for Uma Thurman's role in the *Kill Bill* movies; a very appropriate moniker. The DAP Hawk was the most heavily armed helicopter in any military. There were less than two dozen of them—all designed by and built for the Night Stalkers of the 160th Special Operations Aviation Regiment.

Mick had flown the big helo on a couple of familiarization flights, but he'd always been partial to his Little Bird. Hard not to be impressed by the DAP Hawk's raw power, but he preferred the super-agility of his aircraft. Less maneuverable, he hoped *Beatrix* was being careful while distracting their target. He shouldn't worry, Rafe and Julian were almost as good a team as he and Patty. He worried anyway.

A hard gust smacked him sideways and he yanked up on the collective to avoid eating the frigate's radio mast.

"Hey look! They do still have an Mi-4 helo tied down on their stern. Ooo! Big wave just buried it in spray. Salt water, fifty year old hardware, bad deal guys."

Mick wished he had a moment to look, but that was Patty's job as copilot in situations like this. He actually appreciated the running commentary as she cataloged the ship's features for the recorder that was also capturing the video for later study by whoever cared.

They were playing an elegant trick on the North Koreans. A DEVGRU team—that the public had called by their long abandoned name of SEAL Team 6 for so long that they'd taken to calling themselves Team 6 anyway—had been launched in a boat by the lurking Chinook helicopter. The team was dodging in behind each of the Korean ships, one by one, and performing a death-defying stunt.

The plan, suggested by the SEALs themselves because they were just that crazy, was to partially disable each ship. Not in a dangerous way, in case they hit a big storm on their way home, but enough to be immensely awkward.

When a particularly tall wave lifted the stern of each ship high enough for the rudder to clear the water, the SEAL team would zip forward in their tiny boat. Undetected due to the helicopters playing distraction games around the command bridges, the SEALs would slap a super-epoxied bar of metal to the hull directly in front of the rudder.

The bar extended out alongside the rudder. The result was that the Koreans would be able to turn to starboard without a problem. But if they tried to turn to port more than a few degrees, the rudder would hit the bar and that was it. Any time they came too far off their course, they'd have to go in a full circle to regain their heading.

For the North Koreans to cut the bar, they'd require calm seas, a skilled diver, and an underwater cutting torch. It was a fair bet that they probably weren't carrying the last item, especially as the bars were titanium—light to handle but with an unusually high melting point.

Even if they were able to cut it, they wouldn't be able to hide the bar itself—it would take a shipyard and new plating to remove it from the hull. Three senior captains were about to be in immense trouble.

"The *Beatrix,* she's complete," Sofia updated him.

The tactical display showed that the heroine of *The Fifth Element, Leeloo,* and the *Beatrix* were standing off in case he needed help with distracting his own light frigate, the largest of the three.

# # #

The *Linda* bucked hard, momentarily making Patty float off her seat. She wanted to shriek with delight.

"You a roller coaster boy, Mick?" She leaned forward to brace herself against her flight harness to keep her hand steady on the controls. Still she could barely follow what he was doing. Goddamn, but he could fly.

"Never been on one," his voice remained Mick-steady. He actually flipped the helicopter upside down in a sideways rollover as he shifted from right-side up on one side of the ship to right-side up on the other.

"Wait! What?" Patty gasped for breath as the adrenaline pounded. Her efforts to match Mick's imperturbable calm were a total failure. "Did you...Oh Crap!," a searchlight swung their way, but Mick was no longer there, spinning them off over the ocean's darkness, "...grow up deprived?"

"No coasters in Alaska except the little ones at county fairs."

"Well, we gotta fix that."

"You going into the carnival business, O'Donoghue?" When he slewed across the deck again, Patty could see trouble was coming soon.

"I'm not gonna—"

She keyed the mike. "Sofia. Our boat is arming. Only rifles so far, but they're scrambling now."

"Roger," Sofia called back. "SEAL team needs two minutes more."

"—build one," Patty picked up right where she left off. "I'm getting your butt on the next one I can."

"Gee, thanks."

"My luck you'll be a *sicker.* But it's a total right of passage and you gotta do it. Can you get me right over the deck?"

"Didn't you just say that they're arming?" He moved off their bow.

She flashed the landing light full in their faces down the length of the deck before Mick dodged aside once more.

"Seriously. I've got a special delivery for them."

"Is this something I want to be party to?"

"Absotively! Now do it. Because your only other option is to circle the stern, and you don't want to draw their attention there."

"SEAL Team clear," Sofia announced.

Mick cursed under his breath. It was nice to know he wasn't so perfectly cool all the time.

"The *Carrie-Anne* still has to recover the team and in these seas that could take some doing," she nudged at him.

"Will your *special delivery* buy the SEALs some time?"

"Duh!" Why else did he think she was suggesting it?

Mick played a game of peek-a-boo over the bow: starboard, dead ahead, and port.

Then he yanked up on the collective and slid the cyclic forward. The Little Bird leapt, but she kept a firm grip on the weapon's release she'd pre-rigged back in Anchorage.

He carved a turn back the other way, out of sight below the line of their bow but with her side of the helicopter so close to the waves that she instinctively edged upslope out of her seat. The water was so close that, if not for the g-force and her safety harness, she'd have crawled right into Mick's lap to get away from it.

Exactly amidships, he turned directly for the boat. He climbed sharply to clear the deck and the railings. Armed seamen out on the deck flattened themselves to avoid being hit by his racing helicopter's skids—he was that low.

Damn he was good! She liked that sooo much in a pilot.

Exactly amidships, he went vertical. Directly above the center of the ship's deck, he shot upward rather than crossing the rest of the way to the far side.

It was all she needed.

Patty hit the release.

At her "Whoop! Cargo away!" Mick laid down the hammer again and shot off into the darkness.

Chapter 2

I can't believe this girl!"

"Woman," Patty snarled at him. Mick just grinned as all of the other women around the table joined in on her side. He was in too good a mood to care. Besides, someone had to keep Patty O'Donoghue in her place. She'd been dancing in her seat for practically the whole flight back to Elmendorf-Richardson. Despite her singing the Oompa Loompa song, off-key, for most of that trip, he couldn't begrudge her a moment of it. Though he couldn't believe she knew all the words from *both* Willy Wonka movies, at least the Oompa Loompa parts.

Screw the mess hall. To celebrate, Mick had dragged them all out to the best pizza in Anchorage, or anywhere in his opinion. Moose's Tooth Pub and Pizzeria had been a fixture in his life. They opened when he was eight, and his family had gone on the first night. It had been to celebrate a big first of his own—his inaugural trip on the family's crabbing boat as cook's helper rather than a passenger. The fifty-mile trip from Seward into Anchorage for some amazing pizza had been his reward. Even though he'd now left the family business, this is where he always came to celebrate. It had also been a fixture of his tenure at the university here.

The owners knew him by name and didn't need to remember his reputation. Showing up with a dozen other Night Stalkers ready for pizza and beer for breakfast at ten in the morning hadn't even phased them. Instead they'd tagged them as rowdies, booted them into a back room, and fed them like you might a starving wolf pack—heavily. Too bad that Commander Altman and his three SEALs had, per usual, slipped away immediately after the mission.

The Moose's Tooth was wood paneled, as welcoming on a cold winter night as on a balmy October morning like this one. A table that could seat twenty felt packed with a dozen of them. God these people were so much larger than life. How in the world had he been lucky enough to work with such amazing folk? He'd done something right, he just wasn't sure quite when.

Napier declared the 5E was off-duty, "dark" for twenty-four hours, so they could actually have beer with their pizza. The Night Stalker rule was twenty-four hours from bottle to throttle. As the 160th SOAR was also on 24-by-7 alert status, it was often tricky getting a drink. Just three days ago he'd been given a week's vacation. Then called back in before he'd even reached a civilian airport. That he was now sitting at his vacation destination but on a mission was a little ironic, even for him; though he was sure that Patty would appreciate it.

In minutes the table was covered with Nashville Nachos and spicy Buffalo chicken wings. Several pitchers of beer arrived. Flight jackets were shed and laughter erupted.

The ship facing the *Leeloo* had tried to dodge the Little Bird with hard maneuvering. It had made the SEALs' job harder, getting clean access to the stern. But the joke of trying to dodge a fifteen-hundred *pound* helo with a fifteen-hundred *ton* ship wasn't lost on this crew—even if it had been on the North

Korean captain. He'd been the first to discover that something had changed and he could only go straight or to starboard.

The *Beatrix* was the only aircraft that had been shot at. Connie Davis had silenced the ship's single rifle round with a brief blast of an M134 minigun across their deck. The M134 Gatling machine gun sounded like a very, very angry and impossibly loud chainsaw when it unleashed its three thousand supersonic rounds a minute. It would take a heartier crew than the frigate's to retaliate against such a noise. After that demonstration, Rafe and Julian didn't have to do any hard maneuvering at all. They had simply floated above the deck, out of reach of the North Korean's searchlights, with their running lights on. No one had seen that they were a stealth craft, but all attention had been riveted skyward while the SEALs had worked their magic at the stern.

Connie sat very quietly beside her much larger husband. Big John was almost as cheery as Patty, at least under normal circumstances. Not a chance that he'd keep up with her tonight. Besides, he'd been in the back of the big Chinook helping with the delivery and retrieval of Team 6's boat. He and Jason, the *Carrie-Anne's* ramp gunner, had been soaked with Aleutian seawater several times during the operation, which had dampened their spirits a bit. Jason nursed a beer and John simply sat with an arm around his wife's shoulders and grinned at the banter circling about the table.

Sofia teased and taunted with her usual flair. Zoe, her copilot, nursed a beer quietly. The rest of the four helos' crews were joining in, whenever Patty's boisterous laugh permitted.

"So, I just—" Patty kicked back in her chair exactly aligning her head with a giant cartoon drawing of a moose on the wall behind her, giving herself antlers.

"Nope," Mick hid his snort of laughter as well as he could when he cut off Patty. "You don't get to tell your own story."

He stared her down and she quaffed her beer—then made ready to spit the mouthful at him across the loaded table. He almost made a bring-it-on gesture, but knew that if challenged, she would. Relenting only because he didn't want to be eating soggy nachos, he continued before she could launch.

"There we are," he glanced to make sure that the door was closed at the moment and there were only Night Stalkers and no servers in the room. "SEALs in the water. North Koreans hopping mad all over the deck because all they've seen of me is a glaring landing light. Half the time they were lying on the deck because of the storm."

"And half the time because they thought they'd be smacked by a whirling dervish. Damn but you can fly, Quinn."

Mick raised a beer in acknowledgement and wondered where the compliment had come from; that didn't sound like Patty. Of course they'd been laughing together for the entire flight back. It had been a good moment for them both.

"Seriously," she said in an aside to Sofia who'd ended up sitting at her side. "He was incredible."

What the hell? Why was Patty buttering him up with Sofia? Sure, the RPA pilot was impossible not to look at—how often did a fashion model end up as a 2nd Lieutenant in any outfit? He'd checked online; she had been. Pretty heavy-duty job for a model to go for, but she'd done it. A real case against female stereotypes, as if his matriarchal family line had given him a choice—didn't matter if she was mostly ashore now, it was still Gran's crabbing operation.

Mick had always felt as if he should have the hots for Sofia, and often caught himself watching her and wondering why he didn't. She fit so many of his ideal-woman fantasies, must be something wrong with him. Wouldn't be a surprise at all if there was. He'd been with some fine women over the years, but wherever the target lock inside him was hiding, it had yet to engage and offer the steady tone of a worthwhile focus.

There were two couples in the group, an incomprehensible event in a military company, but it had happened. Major Napier and Captain Delacroix had tied the knot just a month ago. And the two ace mechanics—Connie Davis and Big John Wallace transferred from the 5D—had arrived on the scene already a couple.

Why not a third? But even if it was allowed, Sofia wasn't ringing his chimes.

He wasn't waiting for some perfect woman, apparently not even when he was confronted with one. He just wanted…

And he was staring again—*Goddamn it!* Even doing something as innocent as sipping her beer, she was like a magnet; if you were a guy you just had to stop and watch her.

No one appeared to notice his lapse, except Patty who was wearing one of those way too pleased with herself smiles.

"I was running out of ideas for distractions," he picked up the story again.

Patty's guffaw burst out and got several people laughing along even if they weren't sure why. When Patty O'Donoghue laughed, it was hard to resist joining in.

He managed, giving her a scowl instead.

She smirked, absolutely thinking the joke was on him. He seriously considered spraying a mouthful of beer in her direction but didn't want to catch the innocent Sofia in the overspray.

"And once I get them all riled up, this one," he pointed an accusing spicy chicken wing at Patty as if he was about to jump across the table and bayonet her with it, "she tells me to fly right over the center of their deck. These guys are fishing out rifles and I'll bet that someone was ranging a surface-to-air missile."

"Here comes the good bit," Patty crowed.

"I get her right over the center of the deck and she unleashes this secret cargo she'd rigged in place of two of the Hellfire missiles without telling me."

"You dropped a pair of dummy missiles on a foreign ship of war?" Major Napier jerked upright in his chair.

That had been his guess too. And he'd reamed Patty but good for it before her laugh had cut him off.

Danielle put a hand lightly on Napier's arm. Most of the women were leaning forward in anticipation, most of the guys were leaping to bad conclusions just as he had. He'd have to remember to ask someone why the gender split. Was it that guys had no creativity in combat and women knew that? Or was it because a woman had thought of it? He didn't like the feel of the latter, but suspected both were equally true. Mick decided against asking Patty, she'd get too much smug satisfaction out of answering him and she was smug enough already.

With masterful timing, Patty waited until all the men had calmed back down. Since he was in on the surprise, he could appreciate her sense of theater. It was just as good as her timing as a copilot.

"Nope!" Patty was so pleased with herself that her big laugh twisted into that rare, high giggle she unleashed only on special occasions. She went from classic cheery-caustic O'Donoghue to impossibly cute Patty faster than a Hellfire could crack the sound barrier.

They had to drop the topic when the door opened and the first round of pizzas arrived. A Greek Gyro sausage pie, a Garlic Lover's with blackened chicken, and a High Protein Land—which it had enough meat to satisfy a grizzly bear, and maybe even a Night Stalker.

Once the waiters were gone, and everyone was groaning with pleasure over their first bites, he picked it back up. He'd rather just eat; it had been a long time since his last Moose's Tooth pizza. But Patty deserved her moment in the sun; she'd sure earned it.

"Patty dropped her cargo," Mick said loudly enough to recapture everyone's attention. "It smacked down on the deck and spread everywhere, covering the entire area. As soon as the Koreans recovered from the shock, they were scrabbling about like madmen."

"Caltrops? Those tetrahedral spike things?"

"Marbles?"

"Vegas topless show fliers?"

"A thousand copies of *Playboy?*"

"Better!" Patty crowed as the team tossed out more guesses.

Mick waved his slice of pizza at her for her to take her bow.

"I cleaned out the PX," Patty said it with her voice dropped into mission-debrief neutral. "We delivered a two-hundred-and-three pound payload of...Snickers, Almond Joy, Twix, Reese's—you name it."

"She gave them a taste of what the West can dish out."

The exclamations and laughter rolled around the table.

Mick tipped his beer in a silent toast to her.

He loved her out-of-the-box brain. She was always surprising him with it.

The smile she sent back was beyond radiant.

Damn! There was absolutely no doubt about the accuracy of his earlier assessment. Chief Warrant 3 Patty O'Donoghue was a real looker.

# # #

Patty leaned on Mick's arm, not quite sure how she'd gotten there. She drank so rarely that the second beer had blurred reality long before she'd reached the bottom of the glass. She wasn't even sure she had reached the bottom of it.

She squinted at the sky. The storm-ravaged night raging over the Aleutians had started as a partly sunny day in Anchorage. Above the Moose's Tooth parking lot, a thin haze now turned the whole sky blindingly bright. Squinting behind her sunglasses wasn't helping. Wait, she wasn't wearing sunglasses. Patty found them tucked up in her hair and pulled them down. It didn't help. No matter how she looked at it, it was two in the afternoon—a Night Stalkers' two in the morning—she was tipsy and hanging onto...Mick. That was the most surprising thing of all.

"Ya know," she could feel her voice softening, but she was feeling too relaxed to reel it back in. "I use-ta be able to drink a whole swordfisheryman's crew under the table. Look what's happened to me. Pitiful! The Army has ruined me for life as a lush." She waved a hand extravagantly and almost went down on the parking lot. She held on hard and inspected the surface under her boots. It was just lying there. No ice or snow, not even wet. Nothing to blame it on but herself.

"Just look," Mick said agreeably.

"You don't smile much, Quinn." She squeezed his arm beneath his jeans jacket. "Work out though." Which explained what she was hanging on to.

"I smile plenty."

"Nope! You don't. Looks good on you. Just like the muscles. Sofia would appreciate that. You should smile at her more." She really didn't think it was the beer that was making her this unstable—all she had on was a pleasant buzz. There had to be something else, but she couldn't think what.

"I don't care what Sofia would appreciate on me."

"Sure you do," Patty patted his arm and tried not to giggle at the repetition, but couldn't resist Patty-patting his arm again—it was a very nice arm.

"No, I really don't," he placed one of those big strong fisherman's hands of his over hers to secure her grip on his elbow. He used that link to guide her to the Ford sedan they'd signed out of base transportation for the evening.

She looked up at those dark eyes. His sunglasses were still tucked in his pocket as if all this brightness was somehow normal. He looked serious, but then he always did. Patty knew that if she was even a little drunk, her judgment went to hell. It was like the Joe Nichols song, *Tequila Makes Her Clothes Fall Off*—which was also goddamned country. Her one bout with tequila and she'd lost her virginity to Timmy Thompson. *Timmy Thompson? Really?* It had been enough to make her swear off boys for the whole rest of high school, and tequila for a lifetime.

"But I'm not that drunk."

"Uh-huh," her hunky pilot nudged her into the car's passenger seat. When he leaned inside and reached across to snap in her seatbelt, she seriously considered nibbling on his ear just to make him crazy. But then he might think she was interested in him and that would never do, because he was interested in Sofia and there was honor among women.

"You don't sound convinced about my soberishness."

"You're a lightweight, O'Donoghue. I don't think that you could ever drink a swordfish steak under the table, never mind a boatload of 'swordfisherymen.'"

"I could—"

He cut her off by flipping her door shut and circling around the hood.

She leaned over and locked his door. That would teach him to cut her off.

He raised the key fob outside the window, dangled it in front of her eyes for a moment, and hit the Unlock button. All the stupid doors complied with soft thunks of smug complicity. It was unfair. They all ganged up against her.

"I'm not drunk, I'm just happy," she pointed out once he was in the car.

"Uh-huh." The signature Mighty Quinn grunt.

"It was a good time." It had been. Laughter, pizza, and the relief of another successful mission. The 5E was the first place she'd ever been where her gender hadn't been some awkward barrier. She'd earned her place by kicking ass in a kick-ass team. And tonight they'd really appreciated her for it.

Men like Mick didn't understand how rare and important that was. At least Mick tried, but no guy was ever going to get it. Men were all…

"And you are too interested in Sofia." Was he blockheaded enough not to realize it?

"Nope."

"Of course you are. She smart, skilled, has an accent that could convert the Pope to a life of carnal bliss, and she's drop-dead gorgeous."

"Yep, she's all that." His complacent agreement didn't sit well with her as he drove out onto the Old Seward highway and headed back toward JBER through mid-afternoon traffic.

"Then how come, Quinn?"

"Don't know," his voice went soft. She knew that tone shift. He'd taken her question seriously, so she waited out the long silence before he continued. "By all rights I should be, but she just doesn't do it for me."

"But if that's true,"—and Mick never spoke anything but truth—"why are you always staring at her?" Patty shifted in her seat until she was leaning as much on the door as her seat so that she could look at him. He was watching the road, but concentrating on something in the far distance.

"Partly wondering why I'm not interested in her."

"And the other part?" Mick Quinn didn't open up like this very often. She could only recall him drinking one beer, but maybe it had mellowed him just enough.

"Easy woman to look at."

"Eye candy. God, men are such trolls. What do you see when you look at me?" And as soon as she said it, she wished she could take it back. That feeling of euphoria that had followed her since the pizzeria plummeted away faster than a bomb-load's worth of American candy.

Mick glanced over at her as he turned in at the base's security gate. A smile tugged at one corner of his mouth, but he didn't let it out to play.

"I see a royal pain in the ass."

"Great." Exactly what a *girl* wanted a handsome man to think of her.

"Damned pretty one."

Before she could ask what that crack meant, he had the window down. The MP on duty at the gate was looking in at them and asking for their IDs.

Patty guessed she was pretty enough; at least men always said she was. Maybe they just liked her red hair. And that was the problem with men. They liked doing the looking and that was usually all they cared about. For them the next stage after that was getting a girl to go horizontal without any getting-to-know-you first.

She'd thought Mick was better than that.

He was. She'd flown with him for over two years and there was no question he was. Any thought of Mick Quinn had the word "decent" automatically attached to it as thoroughly as "sexy" attached to Sofia. "Sexy" slid right off Patty O'Donoghue.

But if a guy like Mick didn't want a woman like Sofia, then what the hell did he want?

Well one thing was damn sure—Patty slouched in her seat as he pulled up in front of the JBER transient quarters—she was nowhere in the running at all. Not that she cared or anything, but she didn't like the feeling.

A woman wanted to feel that she was worthy of any man she took a liking to and finding out that she wasn't up to the standard of one of the best guys she'd ever known…sucked! Big time!

# # #

Mick didn't notice that Patty was still in the car until he was a half dozen steps toward the three-story white block structure of Matanuska Hall. He circled back and opened her door for her. She was slumped in her seat, her arms crossed tightly in front of her. It always amused him that angry women didn't understand that gesture only emphasized the shape of their breasts—of which Patty's were a particularly fine example—and distracted men even further from whatever was the matter.

In this case Patty was glaring at the dashboard as if it was trying to kill her.

She been so bright when they left the Moose's Tooth, practically shining from within. He'd seen her drunk a few times and she wasn't in any stage of her manically-inebriated modes, but even dead sober her moods could move fast enough to make his head spin.

By any prior O'Donoghue standards, she'd really shone at dinner. Her magnetic laugh had become the keynote sound of the meal. She'd turned a convivial meal into a party, everyone joining in on the merriment until they were helpless to resist; sometimes helpless to breathe from laughing so hard. She'd gotten Major Napier to unwind enough to tell jokes about some rather unlikely corporals and what had happened when they'd tangled with the wrong woman—a brigadier general's exceptionally comely wife.

Now Patty had apparently decided that the world was a horrid place. Maybe she was too hung over to breath. Her slightly hyper system couldn't have metabolized such a transition in the seven miles they'd driven. Even her notoriously mercurial mood swings didn't account for this. Besides, they were typically variations of cheerful and ecstatic. It was one of the things he'd always appreciated about her; even when she was whining, it was from a place of wry humor.

"Hey."

When she didn't react, he leaned in and reached over to unlatch her seatbelt.

She growled something unintelligible about "such trolls" and then she grabbed him.

One moment he was leaning across her; the next she had him by both of his ears. With a sharp twist—that would have hurt like hell if he'd any balance with which to resist the action—she turned his face to hers.

Then she kissed him.

He'd been kissed plenty enough ways to recognize when it was in anger. Patty's kiss wasn't that—it was vengeance. She kissed him hard, in a cobra strike attack. She drove at him until his lips hurt even when they shifted to a French kiss—accompanied by a deep growl that vibrated between them.

One of his hands found purchase on the steel post of the headrest and he, in turn, drove her back against it. He'd never thought about kissing Patty O'Donoghue, not really, except on really stupid, really lonely nights.

With the choice taken out of his hands, he could absolutely appreciate everything she brought to her attack. The taste of ginger-chocolate cheesecake...the power…the force...the need.

It woke a need in him too. A deep need that rooted so hard in his gut that he finally pulled free despite her tight grip on his ears.

They stared at each other from a breath apart for a long moment.

Then she—thankfully—let go of his ears and slapped her hands over her face to hide her eyes.

"I did *not* just kiss you. Please tell me that I didn't just kiss you. God I wish I was drunk."

"Why?" he answered to buy himself a moment to think. The system-wide shock of kissing Patty O'Donoghue was still roaring through him. Like a helicopter just struck by lightning, it was impossible to tell which of his systems were working at the moment and which weren't.

"Why? You're a blockhead, Quinn. If I was drunk, I could blame that kiss on being drunk."

"But you are, so you can."

"No. Wish I was, but I'm not." Then she did a very unusual thing for her; Patty blushed. Her creamy skin went brilliant red, several shades brighter than her auburn hair.

"Maybe I could buy you a t-shirt that says, *The Devil Made Me Do It.* Would that make you feel better?"

She uncovered one eye and glared at him.

"I could sing you a country song, about the man who done you wrong. Maybe that would help?"

"Aren't you supposed to be angry or something? I'm the one who kissed *you*."

Mick squatted on the pavement and leaned back against the inside of the open car door but he wasn't ready to move any farther away from Patty just yet. He could use a distraction, but the parking lot of on-base lodging was very quiet at two in the afternoon.

He'd never considered kissing Patty for real. And by how flustered she looked, it was clearly something she'd never thought about either.

"C'mon Mick. Talk to me," she uncovered the other eye and then dropped her hands into her lap. "What are you thinking?"

"Thoughts I shouldn't be," which was true. She was a fellow officer, but he was a commissioned lieutenant and she was an enlisted chief warrant—which were supposed to stay worlds apart.

"Slow down there, Mick. I'm not looking to get bulldozed by The Mighty Quinn." He liked that she was already recovering and had her feet back under her, at least metaphorically as she was still buckled into the car seat.

"Wasn't quite where my thoughts were going."

And her face closed down hard.

# # #

Right back into her same angry cave.

She wasn't good enough.

Patty could still taste Mick on her tongue. Could still feel the pressure on her lips that had far exceeded how hard she was holding him. Now she felt trapped between the seatbelt, the central console that ran between the bucket seats, and Mick studying her through slightly narrowed eyes from just an arm's length away. Far more trapped than when he'd been reaching across for her seatbelt and something had made her kiss him.

Oh God! How were they going to fly together? It was the best part of her life and she'd fucked it up. They'd be even closer together than they were right now every time they were airborne. How could—

"My thoughts were going somewhere else entirely."

Yeah, like how fast could he get her transferred. She was going to lose the 5E—

"I'm thinking that if that's how you kiss when you're pissed at the world, what would it be like to kiss you when you were happy?"

—and she'd lose the friends she'd already made among the women of the…

Mick was just squatting there with that damned half smile tugging at his lips. He was…

"Say what?" Patty blinked, but couldn't rewind the statement.

"C'mon," this time he didn't lean in, just reached across her to snap her seatbelt free. Then he rose to his feet and stepped back.

She stared at the offered hand. His face was out of sight, above the line of the car's roof. All she could see was Mick Quinn from mid-chest down, and one of those big fisherman hands held palm up to assist her from the car.

What the hell. Patty took it, figuring she wasn't about to trust her legs at the moment for reasons that had nothing to do with alcohol.

He closed his hand over hers and rubbed his thumb across the backs of her knuckles. It was a question, but one look up at his eyes when she reached her feet made her decide that the question wasn't for her. It was for him.

Without another word, he escorted her to her hotel door… and left her standing there flat-footed.

Mick moved down the hall to his own door, worked the card key, cursed softly, and worked it again. On his third try the door opened and he went in without a single glance back her way; she might as well not exist.

She slotted her own card key, four attempts before she stopped flipping it around and looked at the little arrow mostly hidden by a garish delivery pizza ad. Turning it properly, the door clicked open with much the same smugness that the car door locks had shown.

Okay, maybe Mick was still thinking about her if he couldn't open his own door either.

Because no matter how that kiss had started, the way it had finished meant she was sure as hell thinking about him.

Chapter 3

I was chatting with Stan McCabe over at the Two-Twelve," Major Napier started talking even as he and Mick set their breakfast trays down on the table the 5E had taken over.

They were the last two to arrive. The rest of the Night Stalkers were already crowded around a long table in the Gold Rush Inn Dining Facility. The evening crowd—which was the Night Stalkers' morning—was mostly Air National Guard grunts, though there were some Army fliers and servicefolk mixed in. The Air Force was based down at the far end of JBER and they used other facilities down at that end of the field.

The floor-to-ceiling curved windows showed a view of streetlights in the last of the fading fall light and a heavy drizzle, chill water that had indeed found its way down the back of his collar as he was crossing from the hotel. Interior lights made it daylight bright inside, enough so that he almost pulled down his sunglasses.

Conversations buzzed through the air and sounded off the high wood ceiling. It made the room feel even more crowded and friendly than it already was. The diners all fit a common motif: military wear and military hair.

The Night Stalkers' table had been easy to spot because many of them grew their hair long. If their main customers—SEALs and Deltas—wore their hair long, Night Stalkers took it as permission to fit right in. In this environment, men with hair over an inch long or women with it past their jaw were clearly marked as Special Operations. As such, they were given an especially wide berth by mere mortals of the ANG, Army, and Air Force.

The first thing he'd spotted was the red banner of Patty O'Donoghue's cascade of hair down to her shoulders. Patty was sitting between Rafe the DAP Hawk pilot and Danielle, and being her usual chipper self. She looked as if she'd spent a full twelve out cold and then run a 10K before breakfast or something. Health and vitality poured off her, but down at the far end of the table he couldn't seem to soak any of it in. Nobody looked that good after just four hours sleep. Maybe she was doing it on purpose to rub in the fact that he hadn't slept a wink.

He ignored her smug look when he dropped into one of the last two seats next to Sofia.

Mick looked at his watch. Seven at night, all he'd had since kissing Patty was four hours of staring at the ceiling. And it hadn't made anything make more sense.

Napier was going on about the Two-Twelve.

"Don't you sleep?" Mick tried to slow him down so that his own brain could catch up.

The Major ignored him, so he turned to Danielle. She was the rational one of the couple and had become their natural leader throughout training because of her incredible strategic vision.

"Doesn't he sleep?"

Napier stopped steamrolling them and glared at Mick. Mick really didn't care, he just needed the major to give him a few moments to catch up. And whatever else Napier did, he never interrupted his wife.

"He sleeps only *un petit peu*," Danielle conceded in her soft Québécois French, but her own happy smile said that she wasn't talking about him being off somewhere talking to the Alaska Air National Guard's famous 212th Rescue Squadron.

Which meant that Rapier had gotten even less sleep because he'd also…

Mick wasn't going to think about what her smile implied. He really wasn't. He'd already spent hours trying to figure out what Patty O'Donoghue's kiss had meant. Actually, he'd spent most of the time trying to ignore the high voltage charge the kiss had pumped into him that a cold shower had done nothing to cure.

The Two-Twelve.

He'd think about them.

Should have stuck with them in the first place.

The 212th Rescue Squadron were the busiest pararescue jumpers in the military. Not only did they jump into active-war hot zones to extract wounded, but the Two-Twelve worked the search-and-rescue detail in the Alaska Range. Rescue of the fools who thought climbing the twenty-thousand feet of Denali was something anyone with a rucksack and a pair of crampons could do.

"The Pipeline" to become pararescue took as long as the Night Stalkers' two-years of training. He'd transported these guys on occasion during his time in Afghanistan. Typically the Air Force flew them in, except when they had to go somewhere truly ugly and then they called in the Night Stalkers. Pararescue jumpers were the ultimate badasses. *Because sometimes even the SEALs need to call 911,* and Air Force PJs were who they called.

Napier was setting them up for an exercise with these guys? Oh man.

"I asked the unit's commander to come join us," Major Napier waved a hand toward an Air National Guard major who dropped into the last open seat next to Mick, holding a mug of black coffee.

"Who's the local here?"

Mick ticked up a finger, "Here, sir."

"Hear you got this lot out for some real Alaska fodder at Moose's Tooth. Good man," he landed a solid slap of approval on Mick's shoulder and then grabbed on and shook him back and forth a bit. "Pete said you folks were now looking for an Alaska-style training hike. Excellent!"

Mick swallowed down his own reaction and scanned the table. Other than Napier, they were all in shock. They'd been Army for enough years that it was subtle, but it was there on every face. Napier had promised them twenty-four hours dark—welcome to the Army. It wouldn't be a problem for the members of the 5E. After all, a hike meant they wouldn't be flying and the twenty-four hour bottle-to-throttle rule wouldn't apply.

Last of all he looked at Patty. But she wasn't watching him; she was watching McCabe. And he couldn't read anything into her expression.

# # #

Patty was well aware of Mick's attention and refused to give him the satisfaction of knowing he'd cost her even a minute's sleep. He did look awfully good sitting next to Sofia. Too good. Was that why she'd maneuvered the empty spot to be by Sofia? Because Mick was too good for Patty O'Donoghue?

Damn it! She'd just done it again, except this time she'd done it to herself. Mick was supposed to be her pilot, no more, no less. Well, maybe friend as well, but she wasn't supposed to have kissed him. And she *really* wasn't supposed to be bothered by how amazing a couple he and Sofia made.

At least he looked like hammered shit this morning, as if he'd drunk a pitcher or three rather than a single beer. That made Patty feel a little better. Because she could only think of one reason he'd look that way…he'd slept as little as she had.

ANG Major Stan McCabe gave her the perfect excuse to ignore Mick.

First, he was the poster child, no, the poster *man* of the super-fit warrior. He wasn't the handsomest guy around, not a chance sitting next to Mick, but he was built on an impressive scale. Six-four and all of it muscle; he also had a smile that came out far more easily than Mick's.

Second, Mick had suddenly gone humble when the PJ sat next to him. Mick was always kind and decent, but it wasn't like a member of the 5E to go humble around anyone. But McCabe was a pararescue jumper. Yeah, that made her feel pretty humbled as well.

"We have a team headed up into high country," McCabe's voice was deeper than even Mick's, "for some ice and snow training. We're glad to have you folks along. Don't worry. If you have any problems, we're going up there to practice high-altitude rescue anyway. We're always glad to take on some real-life training opportunities."

For all his easy manners, he'd just thrown down the gauntlet. Patty wondered if Napier was behind that or was it just the normal: one branch of the military baiting another. For herself, the gauntlet hadn't even hit the ground and she'd already grabbed onto it. She knew it was a bad habit, but a challenge was never allowed to slip by Raymond O'Donoghue's little girl. She was going to tackle and take down whatever mess the Two-Twelve sent her way. "Real-life training opportunity" like hell. She'd show them what a Night Stalker was made of, especially a 5E.

"I checked the records," Major Napier began before she could state her acceptance of the challenge. "The last person to do any ice-and-snow work is me, and that was before I joined the 5E. For most of you it was over a year ago."

O'Donoghues were Gloucester fisherfolk, cold didn't scare her a bit. Several of the others were looking unhappy.

"Ready to gear up and go, sir," Patty stated emphatically and glared at Mick, daring him to beg off.

He didn't. Instead, he silently nodded his acceptance which she supposed was better than his trademark enigmatic grunt.

"I don't expect you all to have full ice-and-snow gear with you," Napier surveyed the table, "but Major McCabe has agreed to outfit everyone from the ANG stock. I want you to know that this training is unscheduled and completely optional."

A wave of relief circled around the table. Patty was going to kick Mick's butt big time if he tried to wimp out on her.

"So I expect to see every one of you in ten hours at the Two-Twelve's ready room. Oh-five-hundred tomorrow. You'll receive a full kit at that time." Then Napier ended the conversation by standing up with his finished tray and leaving the table.

"So much for optional," McCabe laughed. "He was a total hard ass when we went through West Point together. Nice to see that some things haven't changed. Any questions for me?"

McCabe refused to give out any details about the training mission itself. "Some hiker gets himself in trouble up on Denali at nineteen thousand feet and the Two-Twelve gets a call. We find out information as we go. Our radioman has a script written by our training director. We only know what he tells us, when he tells us."

"Who's your training director?" Mick asked in a voice that told Patty he already knew the answer.

Oh. Of course.

"Caught me! Love local talent!" McCabe slammed another cheery slap against Mick's shoulder, probably hard enough to shatter your average person. He lumbered to his feet, taking his mug with him. Then he looked up and down the table. "We're running this one as real as possible. You'll want to get some rest."

Patty knew she'd been dumb in a couple of ways and she had to talk to Mick before it grew any worse. She'd apologize for kissing him and any other weirdness she'd created by giving in to that impulse, no matter how surprising the results had been.

But when the table had quieted after their initial reactions, she was still at the far end of the table from Mick.

And he was busy talking with Sofia.

Crap!

# # #

Sofia had Brazil and Los Angeles, both southern climes, for a background. She very quietly confessed her fears about the training mission to Mick in a voice more nervous than he'd credited as possible for Sofia Gracie. Her natural state was one of overt confidence and flamboyance. Vivacious Latina typically poured off her in waves, making the contrast of her present mood all the more startling.

It turned out that her only ice and snow experience had been during a freak storm that had hit Fort Jackson, South Carolina during Basic Training. Her duties were performed in air-conditioned trailers typically thousands of miles from her targets.

Mick felt both deep sympathy and great respect for her. Of all of them, she could have legitimately begged off from the training. An RPA pilot really didn't need to prove Special Operations survival skills. But she'd put that suggestion to rest, fast.

"They will no be leaving me behind. My team she goes? Then I go, too," she tapped a finger sharply above her generous chest. It earned her several surprised looks followed by approving nods from those close enough to overhear her. Sofia's voice quieted again until only he could hear it, "But you must tell me how not to look like the fool. That I not like at all."

So they talked about snow and ice. It was strange, it was like trying to explain Special Operations thinking to a civilian. If they hadn't at least served, there was no common language to explain with.

"You'd die to protect a teammate?" *Duh!* That was a given before the conversation could even begin. Special Operations soldiers didn't sign up for a tour, they signed up for a career.

Over a second cup of coffee he switched from descriptions of mountain weather and snow conditions on glaciers—which was being very hard to communicate and was probably scaring the crap out of her—to teaching her basic survival skills.

"As long as you can still feel your toes and fingers, you're fine. They may hurt or sting like mad, but that's just a warning; you're still okay. It's when you can't feel them anymore that you're potentially in trouble."

"Layer up: thick socks over thin, thin gloves then thick. Take off only the layer you have to and for as little time as possible."

"When walking, spend as much time as possible thinking about keeping your fingers and your toes in constant motion. It boosts circulation and distracts you from the fact that you're freezing your butt off."

And he tried not to think about Sofia's butt as it was an exceptional one. Besides which, this wasn't the woman who'd cost him a night's sleep. He glanced over at Patty…except she wasn't there.

Nor was anyone else. They were the only two left at the table. Someone else had even cleared their empty trays; it was just the two of them and their two long-dry coffee mugs. The Gold Rush Inn was no longer rushing. A few troops were sitting a halfway across the spacious hall. A cleaning crew was moving through flipping chairs onto tables and sweeping the floor.

Outside the window, evening had long since turned to dark night.

"We should get some sleep," he managed in a mumble. He'd never actually been alone with Sofia in the three months since she'd joined the unit. It was a heady feeling to just sit quietly with such a stunning woman. And to discover the thoroughly pleasant and intelligent person that her beauty made so difficult to see.

He rose, and pulled her chair out for her. Easy to admire the way she rose from her seat, too; her simplest gesture reminded him of her surname. Sofia Gracie. Wise Grace, he translated to himself.

Maybe Patty had a point. Maybe he and…

The rain had turned cold, but not bitter, so it wasn't snow. At least not yet. He walked her to her door in the transient lodgings and stood back until he was sure she had it unlocked.

Then Sofia turned to him without moving into the room.

"It is very sad."

"It…what? What is?"

Sofia smiled softly, "It is very sad for me, the way that you are looking at her and the way she is looking at you."

"Who?" But he knew who and felt stupid for even asking. Sofia didn't bother to answer his question.

"We could have a very wonderful time together, I think. But that is all it would be." She leaned forward enough to kiss him lightly on each cheek.

She smelled lush and warm. And he was just tired enough to lean into the moment.

"I do not want to hurt the woman you fly with, so we will leave that idea alone," she said softly in his ear. "I just will thank you for your help this night. I be much safer tomorrow because of you."

Her words were a warm brush across his tired thoughts.

"Now go," she pushed against his shoulder to get him moving down the hall toward his own room.

He stopped at his own door and looked back.

She was watching him and her sigh carried easily down the silent hall to him.

"Ah, what I could do with such a man."

Her words didn't register until her door had closed behind her and he stood alone in the long, darkened hallway.

# # #

Patty hit the Air National Guard's Ready Room at 0430.

She'd heard them last night. Hard not to, she'd been lying awake cursing herself for eight times an idiot and Sofia's door was directly across the hall from hers. Patty had slipped up to the peephole in just her oversized t-shirt and watched them, but could only make out some of their words through the door. Sofia's final sigh and what she could do with Mick sliced at Patty.

But even though she watched for fifteen minutes, and then twenty, Sofia's door had not reopened.

Nor had Mick returned to beg entrance.

Patty sorted and stowed her own gear into a large pack. When she returned from the locker room now dressed in long johns, turtleneck, and other multiple layers, Sofia and Mick had arrived as well. As the ANG's quartermaster issued them gear, Patty could detect no coy looks between them. Mick was always so considerate that it was hard to tell if he was treating Sofia any differently than yesterday, or a month ago.

He didn't treat herself any differently either which was as confusing as hell.

"Hey, Patty."

"Hey, yourself," was her utterly lame response. If he was having issues with her, it didn't show. If he was cozying with Sofia the same night Patty had kissed him, he sure didn't look guilty about it. How was she supposed to know how to act if—

"Vee go now!" Major McCabe roared out in a fake Swedish accent as he rushed into the Ready Room.

"Vee go!" several of the PJs who'd been assisting the Night Stalkers with their unfamiliar gear called back in unison. Some sort of a unit thing.

Patty checked her watch, 0450, ten minutes before they'd been told to even arrive to start preparing. Typical training mission for sure. The 5E had been through enough of those that the full crew was already present and they were all within seconds of being ready despite the premature start.

"We're going high up. Everyone, full snow gear. Put on your Bags."

Patty grabbed hers and started struggling into it. It was a one-piece, dull-green flight suit of fire-resistant Nomex that the quartermaster had issued her along with all of the other gear. Then she began layering snow pants and parka over it.

"We have a climber trapped just below the summit on Mount Hayes at thirteen thousand feet. Exact location unknown.

Conditions: three inches fresh snow last night, seven degrees Fahrenheit, zero at the summit, winds light at ten knots. Storm coming. Go! Go! Go!"

A stream of PJs poured into the room and began yanking pre-packed gear off racks. They were moving fast and even with a head start gearing up, the Night Stalkers were having trouble keeping up.

"Who are my jumpers?" McCabe roared out.

Two of the parajumpers raised their hands and grabbed parachutes from the racks as well.

"Who else? C'mon people, I need two more," Major McCabe's tone made it clear they were going to be Night Stalkers.

Mick looked over at her and raised his eyebrows in a question. Despite what had or hadn't happened yesterday, Mick was asking if she'd jump with him.

The relief that washed through her was strong enough that she didn't even think about the consequences, just shot her hand up.

"You got two," Mick told McCabe.

McCabe gave Mick one of his crippling slaps of approval then pulled down a pair chute-and-reserve rigs.

That's when it sunk in. The winds might be light up on the mountain but at thirteen thousand feet…

It was common knowledge in mountain climbing—a sport that Patty had only participated in as part of her military training—that a thousand feet up was about the same weather change as three hundred miles north. It was October at sea-level in Anchorage. At thirteen thousand feet up…they were effectively going four thousand miles north, somewhere way farther north than the North Pole. Like right over the top and into Siberia. And she'd just agreed to parachute into that?

She looked at Mick.

"And you thought flying into that little rainstorm was nuts," he teased her. But his smile was easy and that he wanted to jump with her—rather than ship her out to another regiment entirely—was enough of a relief that she'd just go with it.

McCabe came over with a detailed map of the mountain.

"Hey, Major," Mick teased him. "You're not trying to kill off the *local talent* are you?"

Patty appreciated his attempt at humor. It was nice to know that Mick was worried as well despite the calm stance he was presenting.

McCabe smiled easily, "Not today, buddy." Then he called over the other two PJs with parachutes.

"This is Two-ton and Caspar the Ghost," and that was the end of the intros. McCabe jabbed a finger at a high valley on the map and spoke quickly just as if it was a real emergency.

"Yesterday we dropped a radio repeater right in this valley, so that's the signal we all are trying to 'save.' But we can't get a helo in there for fear of causing an avalanche: too much noise and wind."

"Say what?" Patty did not want to be jumping into any avalanches. Or having her jump cause one that would then kill her.

"Which we proved by triggering every avalanche we could yesterday before we did the drop. Anything that was going to let go already has."

"Oh, sorry," Patty clamped her mouth shut. McCabe just grinned at her. If it was Mick she'd get revenge, maybe even against Napier, but McCabe was a major and an Air Force PJ so she decided to leave it alone. For now.

"You'll jump into this snow field. The glacier has been stable here for years and we've never seen any crevasses in this area or I wouldn't be sending you in this way. Using the helos, we'll be landing two teams well below you. The higher team will work their way up to you to assist. The lower team will build an extraction route to help you all get back off the mountain in case the helos can't get back in. We lift in five. Let's go!"

McCabe then simply counted off the remaining eleven Night Stalkers into two teams and assigned a pair of PJs to each of them. Sofia ended up in the low altitude team—the farthest from she and Mick. Patty tried not to be pleased by that, but wasn't having much luck.

All of the Night Stalkers, including Napier, Danielle, and Sofia—still exuding sexy despite the "Bag" and heavy winter gear—raced out to the two waiting HH-60G Pave Hawks. The Air Force helos had infrared, a mid-air refueling probe for lengthy searches over remote areas, and two crew chiefs at the side guns. Other than the common Black Hawk airframe, that was all they shared with the *Beatrix.*

The Air Forces' medevac version of the Black Hawks were dull gray in the pre-dawn light rather than stealth composite-black. Broad skis were attached to the wheels for landing ten tons of aircraft on snow and ice. And the cargo bays were rigged to take stretchers and a lot of personnel, rather than large caches of ammunition.

The rotors were already turning as they ducked low and piled aboard. The blades were high enough for safety, but staying low eased the battering rotor wash that was trying to flatten her to the ground out of spite.

Once aboard, Patty checked all of the medical supplies hanging from the insides of the cargo bay and was glad it would be up to a PJ to administer any life saving treatments—most of the bags were marked trauma this and blood that. With what they had stocked here, they could perform some major medical operations while still in flight, and she'd bet when they did that the cargo bay wasn't pretty.

Instead, she stared out at the other helo cranking to life in the darkness and rain, doing her best not to think about it. Mick squeezed in tight beside her, because everyone was squeezed that tight. Not because he wanted to be, of course. But her thinking had shifted a fair ways in the last eighteen hours and she wasn't complaining.

"What did you get us into this time, Boston?"

"Me?" Patty twisted to stare at him planting a fairly hard elbow in a PJ's back by accident. "Parachuting out of a perfectly good helo in the middle of the Alaska Range wasn't my doing. You're the one who..."

His smile was easy and friendly.

She jumped when the cargo door slammed shut.

"You don't think that I would have volunteered on my own," he made his protest in all innocence.

"What? You're the asshole who volunteered us," she had to shout the last as the rotors bit air and took them aloft. Like typical helo jocks—including Mick and herself—their pilots cut hard-banking turns, forcing her to lean even harder against Mick. Which felt good in the same way the kiss had.

"Well, I knew you were going to volunteer because that's just the kind of stubborn girl you are."

He hesitated for her to protest *woman* but she refused to take the bait.

"I didn't want you being *nuts* alone, so I figured that I better join in so that I could save your cute ass."

"Right, like I'm the one who'll need saving." Patty wondered about that cute ass remark. It just wasn't the sort of thing Mick Quinn said under normal operating conditions, or even abnormal ones. "How many jumps have you done?"

"Before or after military?"

"Before?" She wished it hadn't come out so tentatively. She had her Master Parachutist Badge but very little ice and snow work.

"Okay," Mick shrugged, "you caught me. None before."

She punched his arm, managing not to poke the PJ's kidneys this time, and appreciated his friendly laugh.

"But I got my Master here in US Army Alaska. I was stationed with the Flying Dragons up in Fairbanks at the time. They like jumping onto snow and ice. As long as you have your laser pick and your bugaboos handy, you'll be fine."

"You're shitting me." What the hell was a bugaboo in snow work?

"Really?" He turned to one of the PJs. "Hey, Caspar. She doesn't have her bugaboos."

"Aw crap," he slapped at his gear and shrugged. "Got no spares, lady. Good luck with that."

There was something about the way Mick was looking at her, just a little too carefully bland. She fisted his ribs, hard. And her hand came away feeling as if she'd just punched him in the bugaboo. Mick "The Mighty Dozer" Quinn was a hard-muscled man.

Whatever it did to her hand, she'd hit him hard enough to knock loose a chuckle as well. Just wait until she got him down on the glacier. He was going to pay.

# # #

Mick managed a little sleep, but it was only an hour flight to Mount Hayes at the helo's top speed. It was a flight that he wasn't in the pilot's seat for and that was like an itch he couldn't scratch.

Also, Patty O'Donoghue had fallen asleep on his shoulder which was much, much more difficult to ignore. And it wasn't the tickling against his cheek from the bright orange pom-pom on her hat that was so distracting. She slept there like she belonged and it felt just that way.

Sofia smiled at him from the far end of the cargo bay in a kindly fashion. He still wasn't comfortable with what she'd said last night about his feelings for Patty. Patty was…Patty. They weren't lovers. And they weren't supposed to become lovers.

But Sofia had said something about the way they looked at each other. From Patty he'd seen nothing but her typical range of a hundred different emotions racing across her features.

And he'd looked at her how? In some way that Sofia could see and he couldn't.

He hadn't unraveled the puzzle by the time Caspar the Ghost tapped his wrist and held up five fingers.

Mick nudged Patty with a shrug of his shoulder. She blinked at him like a sleepy-eyed cat, once, twice, then wide awake.

Rather than surprise or embarrassment, she stroked a hand where her head had been.

"You've a very comfortable shoulder, Mr. Quinn."

"Welcome to it anytime, Boston." And that thought went in all sorts of interesting directions, most of them involving a half dozen fewer layers of clothes and a warm bed.

He and Patty? He didn't have time to think anything else as they began their final gear checks. As jump buddies, Patty tugged on various parts of his gear and straps, and checked the positions of the parachute release handle and the cutaway in case the main chute fouled and he had to go for the reserve. The dance of her gloved hands over his harness produced visceral shocks like a stream of static electricity—not painful, just surprising as could be.

When he did the same for her, the sensation didn't go away. The harness strap just above her breasts had his imagination on overload about a shape wholly hidden by all her gear. Her brilliant blue eyes didn't watch his hands, but rather his face.

He almost asked what she was thinking.

But he'd either get back some goofball response, or she'd actually tell him, which he wasn't ready for. And if she asked him in turn, there wasn't a chance that he could come up with a coherent response.

Maybe she didn't have an answer either. The increasing roundness of her eyes staring at him from so close made that seem more and more likely. Mick actually took comfort from that; at least that way they'd *both* be in uncharted territory.

"One minute," Caspar shouted and Two-ton opened the big side door.

The blast of cold slammed into the helo and swirled around the cargo bay.

"Holy shit!" Patty left her heavy knit hat on. It had a gold upper half, orange lower half, red ear flaps darker than her hair, and a red-and-orange pom-pom on top. It made her look like a crazed leprechaun or diminutive Alutiiq goddess…too damned cute either way. She yanked a jump helmet over it. He buckled it under her chin as she pulled down goggles. She did the same for him, but there was no time to appreciate the sensations. Besides, it was freezing.

Caspar and Two-ton knelt side by side with their backs to the cargo door. The two big PJs saluted them and then tumbled backwards out the door. That opened up enough space for he and Patty to move into place.

A peek out showed the PJs popping their chutes. Both had good openings on their mains.

They turned their backs to the door and shot salutes to Major Napier; McCabe had stayed back at base to oversee the operation from the ground.

After Mick let go but before he tumbled backward, he spotted Sofia. Her eyes were wide, perhaps in fear. Perhaps in shock at the severity of the cold.

He sent her an encouraging thumbs up.

If she returned the gesture, he didn't have time to see it. Gravity snatched him and he tumbled into the sky.

# # #

Patty didn't have time to wonder at Mick's final signal to Sofia. In seconds she was colder than after an icy Grand Banks wave swept the length of her Gloucester herring boat. They were falling from fifteen thousand feet at over a hundred miles an hour.

The wind chill was horrendous.

And the view was incredible.

It was dawn at Mount Hayes, the sun a bright, deep-red orb rising over the spiky rock-and-ice shrouded peaks of the Eastern Alaska Range. The impossibly rugged mountainscape sprawled in every direction except north. In that direction, the steep slopes tumbled down into a broad river valley where the Tanana River flowed west before the far side of the valley climbed anew up another section of the range to the north. Every peak was lit like a brilliant ruddy torch by the low-slanting sunlight. The valleys still huddled in darkness.

It was impossible to get a visual feel of the distance to the drop zone, everything directly below her was stark white. She pulled her cord while still above Mount Hayes and after the briefest moment—when every parachutist was left to wonder if they had a failed chute—she was jerked hard by the harness.

The deafening wind roar, so loud that she only became aware of it by its sudden absence, made the twenty-mile-an-hour descent rate beneath the deployed chute sound like perfect silence.

A glance up, no line twists, the chute had deployed properly. Down, the two PJs were directly below, still circling in to a landing. To the side, Mick floating along a hundred meters over and fifty below her.

"Always gotta be first, don't you?" she shouted over.

"Just keeping you in your place," Mick hollered back, his voice a faint whisper on the wind. Then she heard him on the radio. "Calling Mayday test on Mount Hayes, can you give us a visual?"

There was a pause.

"You're here! Thank God!" By the high tone of the radio operator in Anchorage, apparently the victim was female. "What took you so long? I'm freezing to death and my leg isn't working right. Hurry please!..." And the operator kept transmitting from the mock victim's radio in a constant stream, totally blocking the radio frequency for anyone else to use. Radios were one-way-at-a-time devices and when the other party didn't shut up, there was nothing you could do.

Patty offered a few choice words that no one else could hear. It drove home a lesson that she already knew—civilians and radio communication were a mix that should never be allowed.

Unable to do anything else, they flew in to land beside the PJs.

Feet touchdown, roll to calf, thigh, hip, twist onto back and shoulder, and end up rolling to sit and face the collapsing chute. Patty was pretty damn pleased she remembered how to do it right. Of course the calculated roll had also turned her completely white by tumbling through the foot or so of loose powdered snow.

The stillness in the high mountain basin was as powerful an impact as the massive wind roar of the jump. She could hear every slick nylon ripple of the collapsing chute, even the paracord sliding through her thick gloves was loud enough to stand out in the silence as she gathered it in.

She could hear Mick's breath, caught between heavy gasps in the thin air and a euphoric laugh at the wonder of the experience. Patty noticed that she was doing exactly the same.

The operator playacting the stranded climber had finally shut up which added to the silence.

"Nice attempt, calling the victim on the radio, Mick," Caspar said as he strode up, his parachute already packed. "And yeah, that babble stream is a fairly typical response. When they do that, jump up two-tenths in frequency. We do that so that we can still communicate with each other. I got a partial directional on the transmitter as we came down. Somewhere east of us."

"Heads up!" Two-ton called out and pointed westward.

Their four packs of gear came down under a single chute, landing well up a ridge in the opposite direction to the distress call.

"Typical McCabe," Caspar commented without much chagrin. "Rope up and let's go."

And that's how their day began, Caspar, Mick, herself, and Two-ton each spaced a dozen yards apart down a common rope line. All walking away from the casualty toward their gear.

"Shouldn't two of us go to the victim?" Patty called out to the lead PJ.

Caspar shook his head and kept plodding along. "Never split up the rescue team if you can help it. Also, if we don't have that gear by nightfall, we'll be the ones who need rescuing."

"It's hard walking away from even a fake victim."

"Yep," was Caspar's answer, but he didn't slow.

Attempts to reach the radio link returned only brief and unintelligible responses. They finally received a clean response, and then Caspar lied that they were on their way.

She supposed that was what you had to tell a victim—and not that you were walking in the opposite direction—but it still didn't feel right.

It took a breathless hour to reach the base of the ridge where their gear had snagged. Unlike most pilots, Night Stalkers spent little time at higher altitudes. Mission profiles were typically below two hundred feet rather than up at thirteen thousand. High flying aircraft were pressurized down to seven thousand feet anyway, but Night Stalkers didn't even have that adaptation. Despite water and aspirin, a steady high-altitude headache thrummed away in the background of Patty's thoughts leaving her feeling muddy and weak.

But she wasn't the only one taking twenty steps then pausing for a rest. Mick was doing the same. She'd wager the PJs could move along faster, but they made a point about the team moving and acting as one.

Patty stared up at the steep, craggy pitch. Blocks of ice tumbled off jagged rocks. High up, their four packs were strapped together and the parachute had wrapped around a particularly large block.

"Which of you two has more ice and snow experience?"

Mick held up his hand.

"Okay," Caspar said. "You're with me. Patty, go help Two-ton fetch the packs. He's good at this. Man moves like two tons of feathers."

Patty stared at him aghast and then looked back up the cliff. Mick was the one with the experience…which is why Caspar had chosen her. *Training mission. Right.*

Mick was close beside her. For just a moment she let herself lean against him and gather strength.

"I won't need any bugaboos for this, will I?"

His chuckle warmed her as much as their contact.

"Not for this, no," then his face darkened as he stared up at the terrain. "You be damn careful up there, Patty. Do exactly what he says."

"Yeah, roger that."

Coming back dead wasn't on her mission profile today, but she hadn't liked that look on Mick's face. Two-ton handed her a second ice axe and then unsnapped the safety rope that had connected her to Mick and snapped his own in its place.

"You've got first pitch." It was the first words she'd ever heard him say. Rather than being gruff, he spoke with a simple confidence that of course she could do this.

Patty scanned the steep ridge face again and picked out a route that would keep clear of the worst of the ice. She indicated her planned route with the point of her ice axe.

Two-ton nodded and, resisting the urge to look back at Mick once more, she led off.

# # #

Mick had trouble keeping his eyes off Two-ton in his yellow parka and Patty in her red one as they crawled upward. A two hundred foot high ice-and-rock field wasn't much of an issue. One at twelve thousand feet atop an Alaska mountain in October was a whole different matter.

"Got it bad, brother," Caspar dragged Mick's attention back down from the climbers.

Mick shrugged. It was the only answer he had.

Caspar started leading him across the glacier, climbing the steep ice field on a slant. Mick followed. He was ten minutes out, just looking back to spot Patty's red parka—still in the lead up the ice face—when he heard a soft cry.

He turned in time to see Caspar go shooting by him.

"What the—"

The rope snapped tight on Mick's harness and flipped him off his feet. Some piece of training must have remained lodged deep in his subconscious. Even as he tumbled to land face down in the snow, he had his ice axe braced high against his shoulder, with his free hand clamped over the head of the axe.

With a twist he managed to roll face down in the snow which jammed the point of his ice axe into the flying hillside. He spun from head first to feet first as the pick dug in. Then he lifted his hips so that all of his weight was driven down onto his crampon-clad feet and the point of the axe by his shoulder. But he didn't lift so high that the rope bearing Caspar's weight could flip him onto his back again.

He scraped to a stop and simply stayed there with adrenaline surging through him.

Caspar, the thought punched through.

Caspar had fallen.

Mick had to—

"You gonna lie there all day, Mick?" Caspar spoke from about a foot away.

"You're—" then Mick knew. "Training fall. Got it. You secure?" He asked the question out of protocol, ignoring the fact that Caspar was standing rock stable beside close him.

"Secure," Caspar reported dutifully. "Long furrow, but not too bad."

Mick eased up and stared at the path his body had plowed through the snow. He had been slow on the arrest. Because he'd…been watching Patty instead of his climbing partner. He knew better. Trust your team, even when they weren't roped to you. Well, he wouldn't make that mistake again.

"Interesting problem, isn't it?" Caspar started coiling the line the ran between them.

"What?" Mick rolled over until he was sitting in the snow.

"Women. Never figured 'em out myself. My ex- had a few words to say about that, I can tell you."

Mick looked up at the red parka. Patty was at a dead stop about three-quarters of the way up. They were far enough away that he couldn't be sure, but she appeared to be looking at him.

Well, that worked, because he sure couldn't stop looking at her.

# # #

"What's up with him?" Patty asked Two-ton, though she learned that the man rarely responded to her questions unless they were about technique.

She waited as if she expected an answer, because she certainly couldn't move at the moment.

Her attention had stayed on the climb.

Two-ton wouldn't accept less. He'd shown her how to pick a foothold in ice. How to give just the slightest bounce to test each placement of foot, hand, or axe—it stressed the position just a little and if she paid attention, she could feel if it was weak.

Twice he'd led her back down over a tricky passage to show her the challenges of a descent. Twice she'd had to ascend by new routes.

It was astonishing how much information he imparted with every soft-spoken suggestion. They could have reached the packs and returned by the time they were three-quarters of the way there, but it was totally worth it.

Then she'd stopped to rest a moment and look around.

At that instant, Caspar's parka-yellow figure tumbled down the slope. Mick's orange had shot off his feet. They'd fallen fifty yards before Mick did some kind of strange flip and twist that jerked him to halt.

The slam against his harness must have been brutal as he stopped Caspar.

"They're in trouble!" she'd shouted. "We have to go help!"

All Two-ton had done was hold up a finger indicating she should wait.

Caspar-yellow climbed back up the slope to an unmoving Mick-orange.

He's hurt! But this time she managed to keep the cry inside her own head.

Then Mick rolled over to sit beside Caspar. After a long minute, they began walking up the slope of the glacier again.

"God damn them!"

Two-ton offered his first smile of the whole day then waved her to continue upward.

She glared up at the packs still fifty feet above them and set off.

No way she was going to look again. For one thing her nerves couldn't take it.

When she reached the packs, it was pure chance that she just happened to see Caspar and Mick glissading down the slope on their butts, using the tips of their ice axes like rudders. Boys! She turned to tie a lowering rope onto the packs.

Hell with her nerves.

Her heart couldn't take it.

# # #

Mick had thought to keep the pace slow to favor Patty, but he needn't have bothered. The hard work of slogging through the snow at altitude slowed him down plenty as well. He might have gone faster, but the PJs set up a slow but steady pace. Breaks were few, conversation light, but neither were they exhausting themselves.

Back at their landing site, they had to poke around to find where they'd stashed their parachutes. A high, thin cloud cover had moved in and flattened the light, the deep furrow of their out-bound path through the knee-deep snow was almost invisible on their return journey.

He gathered in loops of the rope until he and Patty were walking closely together and could speak slowly between deep breaths.

"Of course, I'm doing okay, Meathead," which told him she really was doing fine. "You're not the only fine Special Ops soldier on this mountain."

"Some of us are finer than others, O'Donoghue." Too late to take the words back, he could only hope she didn't interpret them the way he'd been thinking them. Her form may have been hidden by layers of winter gear and little more than her eyes and nose showing between hat and scarf, but she was indeed very fine. Half a head shorter and half the weight of any of the men, she was still moving lightly despite the hard work and heavy pack.

"Fine, huh?"

Of course she hadn't missed it. As they'd been crossing the snowfield, she'd shifted a long way in his thoughts as well. That final image on the helo, Patty O'Donoghue asleep on his shoulder, was causing him definite problems.

"You gonna elaborate on that, Quinn, or just leave me to speculate?"

With Patty, an elaboration could lead to a hundred more banters and ripostes, which he didn't really have the air for. "Speculate away."

They began ascending a ridge which robbed them of what little breath they had. Before they hit the really steep section, they had a gear break to tighten their crampons.

A two-minute task in the training room became a ten-minute ordeal at altitude. The strap to tighten the spikes to his boots couldn't be easily worked because they were now clogged with snow; he had to strip off his thick outer gloves to clear them. Rest a glove on the snow and it disappeared into the powder, making him dig around blindly until he found it.

When he was done, his ice axe was nowhere to be found, until he remembered the tether that still attached it to his wrist. His thinking was slowing down as well.

When he finished, Caspar was squatting in the snow in front of him. "Last time you ate and drank something?"

Mick looked at his watch. Too long. Saving his breath, he answered by digging out an energy bar and his canteen…and almost lost the other glove. He felt less foolish when he saw Patty doing the same.

"High altitude and dry cold dehydrates you faster than crossing a desert."

Mick nodded, he knew that; had heard it in any number of survival lectures. But now he *knew* it.

"Now repack your canteen with as much snow as you can. Then tuck it inside your jacket near your chest to melt it. Do that every time you drink. You know not to eat the snow?"

Mick nodded. It was just asking for lip and mouth blisters, and crashing his core temperature.

"If you ever fall through ice and have to get dry fast, did you know you can scrub yourself with powdery snow. It's so dry that it will absorb most of the moisture."

He hadn't known that one.

Caspar chatted amiably about different uses and conditions of snow for several minutes as if they had nowhere better to be. Another five minutes and Caspar saw whatever he'd been waiting for in his and Patty's faces, "Let's move before you chill down."

Caspar led off again.

"Still glad you jumped, Boston?"

"With you, Quinn? Always."

She drifted back along the rope lead to leave him to speculate on her meaning.

# # #

Tracing the small squawks and radio burps of a weakening signal, they finally located the radio repeater in mid-afternoon.

Except there wasn't one victim, there were two, a fact that the "panicked survivor" had failed to mention in her script. Patty stared down at the two life-size mannequins lying in the deep snow. One had a label on its jacket listing symptoms: broken leg, advancing hypothermia, semi-conscious, can't arouse for over fifteen seconds. The second label was far more grim: DOA. Dead On Arrival.

The steady-paced PJs exploded into action. In seconds they had an IV running into an artificial vein. Caspar tucked the IV bag deep inside his own clothes to keep it warm.

"IV is the best way to raise their core temperature quickly," he explained a piece of information that Patty hoped she never needed to know.

"No hot packs on the extremities. Her heart is barely maintaining core functionality. If we warm the extremities, it will draw critical blood away from the core and flush ice-cold blood back in its place."

Way more than she wanted to know.

"Build up a pair of stretchers."

"A pair?" Patty knew the answer as soon as she asked and turned away to fish the parts out of her pack before they could make an idiot of her by answering. *Leave no soldier behind.* It was instilled in all Special Ops teams ten times more than standard units. They all still said *no man* but they'd catch up soon enough if she had anything to do with it.

Her own reaction to her question was a burning behind her eyes and deep in her heart. It didn't matter that they were mannequins. They were too late for one and possibly for the other. And she'd hesitated. In combat, that could get both her and her pilot killed. Hesitation had been trained out of her long ago—or so she'd thought. Many lessons up on this goddamn mountain today.

Maybe she could blame the environment for her momentary lapse.

During their search, the temperature had dropped below zero. Any hint of sunlight was gone, masked by dark clouds and snow flurries.

"Gets real awfully fast, doesn't it?" Mick knelt next to her in the snow and she felt a little better.

All she could manage was a quick nod.

In unison they both dug into their packs for the rolled-up stretchers. The thick plastic sheet unrolled reluctantly with the cold.

"Load the DOA first," the PJs continued working on the "survivor."

Mick helped her lay the dead mannequin on the first plastic sheet. Pre-attached straps pulled the sides and ends together until the mannequin was cocooned in a toboggan with fore and aft towing harnesses.

When Mick covered its face by cinching down the parka's hood, it was a little too final for her.

Patty pulled both gloves off one hand and rested it on the mannequin's heart. She wasn't the praying sort, so she simply rested her hand there for a long moment and tried to give thanks that this wasn't a real person.

Mick was watching her closely while she pulled her gloves back on.

"What?" It came out harsher than she intended.

"You've got a soft spot in you, O'Donoghue."

"So?" Her defenses were cranked up way too high.

"So, it's both unexpected and sweet." Then Mick kissed her on the exposed tip of her nose before turning to prepare the second stretcher.

She didn't want to wipe it off, but the moisture was cold. The moisture coming out of her eyes was hot and didn't wipe away so easily.

Chapter 4

"*We've got to make* camp," Caspar declared and Mick couldn't agree more.

The snow was falling hard and visibility was rarely more than a fifty feet. They'd made it down from thirteen- to ten-thousand feet before daylight failed them, but there was no chance of a helo evac.

The two other climbing teams were still too far below them to connect up. The mid-level climbing team had been stopped by a bad icefall and forced to break trail wide around it. The lower team had reached the starting point of the mid-level team but that was all.

Command deemed the "survivor" to be sufficiently stabilized that it wasn't worth the risk of a nighttime descent. Everyone would be spending the night on the mountain and they'd all link up in morning.

There wasn't any such thing as a level spot at ten thousand feet up the side of Mount Hayes, so they dug platforms deep into the snow. The two tents ended up fifty feet apart, too far to shout in the rising storm, but they all had spare batteries for their radios, making communications a non-issue. With the "corpse" parked on the far side of the PJs tent and the "survivor" in the tent with the two men, Mick and Patty might as well be on an entirely different mountain when they slipped into their own tent.

"Cozy," Mick observed after flicking on a headlamp. The tent was big enough for two sleeping bags and their packs, as long as they were very close together. It was tall enough to sit up along the midline…barely.

"Sure," Patty agreed readily. "Way better than a Bahamian beach and a piña colada. I thought we left this storm in the Aleutians." He wasn't going to think about Patty in a bikini with a tropical drink in her hand—an image he was finding way too easy to imagine…especially one of those skimpy ones with a red floral print and...

"Yeah," he forced the image to the background of his thoughts, because it certainly wasn't going away. "You think raining on Anchorage would have tired the storm out." Instead it appeared to have riled it up. Despite the deep snow shelf that protected their tent and being on the lee side of the mountain, the wind still slapped the plastic of the tiny tent with sharp snaps and the rattle of ice crystal clouds blown like gunfire against the nylon.

By the light of his headlamp, they jostled and bumped each other constantly as they lay out insulating pads and sleeping bags. Shedding boots was easy, but getting out of the winter gear was far more difficult in the tiny space. They had to help each other and stripping clothes off Patty O'Donoghue was suddenly something Mick didn't want to stop.

With a deep breath and more control than he knew he had, he managed to stop when he reached the "Bag." Even in a shapeless green flight suit that was a couple sizes too big for her, he found a sudden and surprising need to drag her down onto the sleeping bags and try out that kiss again. Topped off by the ridiculously cute red, orange, and gold hat only made the image harder to resist.

Instead, he slid down deep into his own sleeping bag. The tent was warmer than outside, but it was still icy enough to see his own breath. He propped his headlamp in the corner, shining upward. It was disconcerting to watch the thin tent fabric slap so violently above them, but it made for a softer light. He began sorting through their dinner options that had been stuffed in his pack.

"Shredded Beef in Barbeque Sauce, Brisket Entrée, Mexican Style Chicken Stew, or Pork Rib," he read off while flipping through the Meals-Ready-to-Eat packets.

"Vegetarian Cheese Tortellini, Vegetarian Taco Pasta, Vegetarian Ratatouille, or Lemon Pepper Tuna," Patty sounded thoroughly disgusted. "I'm going to kill the Two-Twelve's quartermaster when I get back to Anchorage. If I get back to Anchorage." She buried her face in her parka that she'd fluffed into place as a pillow. "I can't remember the last time I was this tired."

"Here," he fanned his selection, "take your pick."

If it was a rug, he would definitely have gotten a burn from how fast she yanked the shredded beef out of his hand. Well, it was the best choice, which would teach him not to make his own selection first. He went for the chicken stew as a close second.

They talked about the day for the ten minutes that the heaters bubbled away warming up their meals.

Silence, other than the roaring wind and snap of the tent, descended as they packed away the calories.

It was comfortable and Mick was slowly relaxing, glad to finally be mostly warm and out of the unrelenting wind.

He was most of the way through his entrée when he noticed that Patty was watching him. Side by side in their bags they were closer together than in their Little Bird helicopter cockpit. It was easy to see that some question was bugging her.

"So ask already."

She shook her head and the ends of her hair where they stuck past the knit cap slipped down to hide her face.

"You've never been a coy one, Patty. Doesn't work for you, so what are you wondering?"

"Not my place."

What wouldn't be her place to ask?

"Christ, Mick. Are all men so thick-headed?"

He shrugged a maybe and munched on a few cheese-filled pretzels to buy himself some time.

"Sofia?"

"What about her?"

Patty put her face back down in her crumpled parka and released a loud scream of frustration.

"I already told you I wasn't interested in her." Though he did recall that moment in the hall when she'd been so close, so warm, and so kind.

"You talked together for three straight hours last night."

"Three hours? Really?" He'd lost complete track of the time.

"You still insist you're not interested in her. What kind of an idiot are you?" Patty threw one of her peanuts at him, which bounced off his forehead. She picked it up from where it fell on his sleeping bag and ate it.

"Based on the tone of your voice, apparently a complete one."

She cleaned up the remnants of her meal and slipped deeper into her sleeping bag until little showed other than her blue eyes and her orange pom-pom.

He let the silence stretch.

"Fine! I'll kill myself with embarrassment later. What did you two talk about for so long?"

"Oh, ice and snow."

"Ice?"

"Uh-huh."

"And snow?"

"Yep."

"You sat with a gorgeous woman for three hours and all you discussed was ice and snow? What's next? Water? Or were you going to jump straight to steam? And why didn't you jump straight to steam?"

"She's never been exposed to either snow or ice before. Sofia didn't know the first thing about survival in winter conditions. No mountain training for RPA pilots."

Patty whistled and her unreadable expression shifted to one of surprise. Then something that might have been respect. "And still she came along on the exercise. Brave woman. Another thing to like about her."

"Uh-huh," he wasn't going to get back into the conversation with Patty about why he didn't want Sofia.

"I'll be damned."

She mumbled it to herself so he decided that silence was the safest policy. He finished the last of his Wet Pack Fruits side dish and then slid deeper into his own bag once the trash was stowed.

"What else did you talk about?"

"The way we apparently look at each other."

"You and Sofia?"

He shook his head and wondered why he'd said it out loud. He tried to speak his answer, but wasn't sure he wanted to have such a clear gauge of his own reaction. So he pointed from his face to hers and back.

"You and me?"

He nodded.

"And then?"

"And then she booted me down the hall."

# # #

Patty pulled the sleeping bag over her head. It was hard to think when Mick was watching her with those big, dark eyes from so close beside her.

Maybe this was her moment to die from embarrassment. She'd thought…suspected…conjured so many stupid-ass scenarios of those two that even for her it was pretty spectacularly bad. Maybe—Patty was just an idiot beyond belief.

Mick had talked with the beautiful Sofia about ice and snow?

And how he and she looked at each other? But there wasn't anything between them.

Well, nothing except one rockin' kiss.

"Hello in there," Mick pulled up a corner of her sleeping bag.

She grabbed the edge and pulled it back down.

Patty could feel him toying with the pom-pom that must be sticking out, but she'd have to scoot farther down in the bag to pull it inside with the rest of her. That was actively running away from the problem rather than just hiding from it and she couldn't stomach doing that.

How had she ended up in a tiny tent alone with Mick Quinn on top of an Alaskan mountain? It wasn't like she could go down to the weight room and pump iron for an hour the way she had while trying to burn off the aftereffects of that first kiss.

The way *she* and Mick looked at each other?

If she was going to be honest with herself—and she hated to do that under normal circumstances, which these definitely weren't so she'd give herself a break this one time—she certainly *had* been looking at Mick that way.

He was still playing with the pom-pom.

So what if she had? A girl was allowed to look, wasn't she?

She stuck her head back out of the bag.

"What's wrong with me looking at you? It's not like you're grotesque or anything."

That's when he kissed her.

Unlike her own kiss that had been about heat and anger and men being such total and absolute idiots, Mick's was soft and gentle.

Not testing.

Not demanding.

Just a kiss designed to blow her pulse rate off the charts. A kiss that simply *forced* her to slither one arm out of the sleeping bag so that she could wrap it around his neck.

He didn't break off, didn't check in with her, didn't have a goddamn doubt in the world. How freakin' male was that? Her thoughts were trying to scurry off and scatter in a thousand directions and Mick Quinn had them anchored solidly in place with a kiss that had already forced her to scrap any nav charts she'd ever built about men. This was way better.

When he did finally move, it was to kiss her eyelids closed, a motion so gentle it was like a whisper.

And then a peck on the tip of her nose.

The sigh that slipped out of her was wholly un-Patty-like.

Her thoughts again tried to coalesce, but they only managed to offer up one lucid thought.

"Don't stop now, Quinn. You're on a roll."

When he at long last shifted down to nuzzle her neck they ran into problems with sleeping bags and flight suits. There was definitely too much fabric between them.

"You know," she whispered as she toyed with his longish black hair. "These sleeping bags are designed to zip together. In case one of us has hypothermia or something."

After a few chilly moments, the sleeping bags were zipped together, their flight suits and long johns were down by their feet to keep them warm, and it was the last time she was able to speak coherently. After a while, she didn't even try. Instead she concentrated on keeping the joined sleeping bags up over their heads and Mick as close as she could.

# # #

Mick had made love to women in odd places before.

He'd lost his virginity in his bunk aboard the family crabbing boat while it was tied at dock. He and Wilma Cutter, the boat's cook hired on when he'd gotten old enough to work the lines, had multiple trysts there. They'd also used the galley a time or twenty at sea where the storm waves did most of the work for them. And any other place they could find.

Her send-off to college—which had also been her pre-agreed Dear John because though he was staying local at University of Alaska ROTC program, she was off to Berkeley—had been particularly memorable. She'd taken him to her uncle's cabin near the Artic Circle where they'd made love for as long as the sun was above the horizon…most of twenty-two straight hours.

Since then he'd found willing women in war zones, on Italian beaches, and in the back of a British Challenger main battle tank—a very flexible Company Sergeant Major who had offered an exceptional fringe benefit during a US-UK joint training exercise.

But the upper slopes of Mount Hayes was definitely the most surprising.

It wasn't the location and the circumstances; it was the woman in his arms. As with everything she did, Patty O'Donoghue was enjoying herself completely. Rather than being coy, she threw herself at him.

Every time he touched her it elicited a hum or purr of pleasure. When he did something she particularly liked, she made sure he knew it. Most women left it to the man to guess what they wanted, a mystery to be discovered and learned. And a complaint if he didn't figure it out.

Not Patty.

"Hey, cut that out. Oh God! That! Yes! Do more of that! Never, ever stop doing that!"

Making love to her was neither a quiet nor a languid act; it was an incredible, joyous sport.

When he finally cupped her, she yelped loud enough that he wondered if the distant PJs could hear her despite the storm, then she pressed herself into his palm with a happy burble into their shared kiss.

If only he had—

"You really are a meathead, Quinn." Patty stuffed a foil-wrapped condom into his hand.

"I didn't think that I'd be—" Dear God! Patty was giving back as good as he'd given. Her long-fingered hands explored and caressed while he hesitated.

"My oh my! No wonder you're called The Mighty Quinn."

He kissed her again because he really didn't want a running commentary and he did want to taste her again. He couldn't get enough of how she—

Finally she pulled away, "Now, Quinn. For crying out loud, now!"

He sheathed himself and slid into her heat, doubly powerful when compared to the cold wind raging so close by. Her body was exceptionally conditioned as only a Special Operations soldier ever achieved. And she knew exactly what to do with it as she gave him more pleasure than he'd ever found with another. He did his best to return the favor and she flew in his arms until they cried out together.

He was wholly spent when the last of the ripples slid along her slender frame down to where they were anchored together, by his need and her legs hooked behind his.

Unable to stop himself, he wholly collapsed down on her, past even propping himself up on his elbows. Missionary was about the only position permitted by the two sleeping bags and he couldn't find the energy to roll them onto their sides.

Patty giggled in his ear as she held him close.

"Damn but you're good at this. If only I'd known how good. Quinn?"

"Uh," was the best he could manage.

"I can't believe how much time we've wasted not doing this."

"Give me a break, Patty. We do that again and I'm a dead man."

"Hmm," she clamped herself more tightly about him as if his death by superior sex would be a small price to pay.

At the moment he wasn't sure he'd argue with that conclusion.

He did finally manage to find his elbows and lift some of his weight off her, far enough away that he could see her by the light that came in through the small gap at the top of the sleeping bags.

Her smile was huge, he expected that it mirrored his own. Her fine features, slightly bruised lips, and just the hint of the long line of her neck were visible. And her sparkling blue eyes. He'd always thought that to be a ridiculous cliché, but he was looking right at her eyes and that's exactly what they were doing. Her beautiful red hair remained mostly covered by her ridiculous knit hat, the only clothing she still wore other than thick woolen socks that presently had their heels pressed into his butt.

He yanked the hat down over her eyes because the joy in them was too dynamic, like an avalanche coming straight at him, and he kissed her.

Her kiss was so sweet, that he knew he was gone. Acerbic, funny, joyous, and beautiful. What wasn't to like about her?

Then he laughed, a single bark. Wasn't it just two nights ago he was thinking whoever Patty became attached to was going to need all the luck in the world to survive?

"What?"

He kissed her again to distract her, because no way was he answering that question. It wasn't a question of who Patty latched onto; it was a matter of who was lucky enough to get her. And somewhere between teasing a North Korean frigate and camping on an ice-cold mountainside, it had turned out to be him.

Mick let himself sink back down on her, because there was no way he could get enough of Patty O'Donoghue.

Chapter 5

Patty shrugged on a parka so that she didn't freeze when she straddled Mick Quinn for "breakfast."

The PJs had called on the radio, "Half an hour to first light. Be ready to go." The call had been the only sound on the mountainside. The storm was gone and the silence was vast.

She'd unzipped the upper half of the sleeping bags to get some maneuvering room and took a moment to admire Mick's chest by the soft light of the headlamp she'd flicked back on. A man was so differently shaped when he'd been born to hard work rather than when he developed it as a gym workout. Mick's chest was spectacular even by fisheryman standards.

Patty leaned down to rub her own chest over his. The powerful sensations of last night hadn't been diluted by a night sleeping in his arms. Well, mostly sleeping. She'd spent part of it awake and watching him in the darkness as the storm quieted. There hadn't been anything to see in the pitch darkness, but she'd listened to his breathing, felt the rise and fall of his chest where her arm lay across it.

That he was an amazing lover wasn't a surprise. Her own intense response to his slightest touch had been a very pleasant surprise. So often she felt that she ultimately didn't satisfy the men she was with, but Mick couldn't have faked the joy he took from her. The joy they took from each other. Maybe the problem hadn't been with her, but with the men she chose. A comforting thought. And if it *was* true, she'd chosen a home run this time.

Was it going to change things between them? She hoped not. Let them both revel in the glorious sex until he tired of her or she of him. Then that would be settled between them and they could return to just flying together. If this flew the course of her normal relationships, it would be over and gone before command could even begin to care. They'd just stay under the radar while it lasted.

But oh! The way he felt in the meantime.

Finally she'd been lulled back to sleep until the radio had awakened her. The call had only shifted Mick from asleep to groggy.

She'd teased him half awake, and sheathed him. His eyes had fluttered open slowly, definitely not a morning person. He cupped her cheeks and pulled her into a kiss.

Now his body was awake enough and with a judicious shift of her hips, she slid him into her. There was a deep grunt of pleasure transmitted through their kiss and it tickled right down inside her.

"Not much time," she whispered.

"Okay," and he didn't waste a second of it. He drove up into her with a power that flooded her system with happy nerve signals trying to blow their little circuit breakers. She and Mick were rooted together at hip and mouth. He had one hand clamped on her butt and the other holding her hand where she had it pinned next to his shoulder. Under the warm cloak of the parka they pumped, thrashed, climbed, soared, and with a shared moan that ripped from somewhere deep inside them, the dam broke and the waves of heat pounded through her.

"Never freeze to death. As long as." Her heart was racing so hard and the aftershocks crashing so hard that she couldn't get enough air to complete the sentence in one go. "We can find a way. To do that."

He slapped her butt lightly. "Let's go," long before she was ready to shift off him, but he was right.

She sat up, still straddling his hips, and began dressing.

Mick lay on the sleeping bag a few moments longer like a dead man, except for the rise and fall of his chest as the skin rapidly goose-bumped because she'd taken the sleeping bag with her. And his dark eyes tracked her slightest motion.

Undressing together last night had been an awkward and self-conscious act in a space far too small for the purpose. This morning, dressing was intimate and fun.

She wiggled into her thermal underwear, then yanked up the shirt's hem to flash a breast at him.

He grinned and she slapped away his hand when he reached out to caress. Mick was much more insistent about leaning in to kiss her breast and she was only too happy to give him his way.

"You are so good at this," she finally pushed him away and continued dressing. "Whatever woman trained you, I want to shake her hand."

"I have a good imagination," he grumbled though she could see there was someone back there he was thinking of. "Though my imagination wasn't good enough when it came to you, Patty."

"Was that a flirt? From Mick 'The Mighty' Quinn? Shocked I am. Shocked!"

He brushed a finger along her cheek. Just that slight contact was almost enough to have her collapsing back into his arms, especially as he was still lying there naked and beautiful.

"Shocked," she managed in a soft mumble that sounded dangerously like a girlish giggle of contentment.

When he began dressing, Patty managed to suppress a very womanly sigh of disappointment. It was okay, there would be a later. There had to be. A smart woman didn't use a man like Mick

Quinn just once or twice and throw him away. Whatever her other shortcomings, Patty knew smart was one of her strengths. Too smart for most guys.

That thought surprised her enough to make her stop while working her way into snow pants over her green flightsuit.

Had that been the problem?

She was Special Operations which meant she was smarter than the average soldier, but also than the average guy. Mick Quinn wasn't average. He was a Night Stalker, too. Even more, he was an officer Night Stalker. That meant he was damned motivated and twice as smart, and that was completely aside from his stellar flying.

Not only did he keep right up with her jokes, but he also encouraged her when she thought out-of-the-box. Like the candy drop on the KPN frigate. She hadn't needed to explain how fractious it would be to have all of the sailors of their largest ship going on to their mates back in North Korea about the wonders of Western candy. He'd trusted her idea without knowing what it was and then lauded it to others afterward, once she'd told him what she'd done.

She'd always gone for guys who looked like Quinn, or close enough, which in retrospect had been pretty damn shallow of her even if it usually proved to be very fun. But not a one of them had thought like Quinn or treated her so well.

"Here, eat this, Boston." He shoved an opened and heated MRE into her hands. Vegetarian Cheese Tortellini for breakfast, could be worse.

While they chewed, they finished dressing and packing everything inside the tent. Finally it was down to just themselves and two packs.

"You ready?"

"Sure, let's get off this little hill."

"Bundle up."

"Why? Storm is gone. It's so quiet that the helos will probably just pluck us off the hillside."

He laughed in surprise and then amusement.

"What?"

"Have you been a little short of breath this morning?"

"I thought that was the sex."

"It was," he kissed her and she'd never get enough of that. The way she went so unexpectedly soft inside every time he did was just...weird. Wonderful, but weird.

Then he yanked down her hat and pulled her parka hood over it. He snapped a rope into her harness and his.

"There is another reason."

# # #

Mick unzipped the tent carefully, battering at the snow so that it didn't pile into the tent.

He heard Patty's gasp behind him, but he made himself concentrate. He didn't know how deeply they were buried, or what he'd find at the surface. Packing the snow off to either side, he tunneled upward. He was past kneeling and up to a crouch before his hand finally broke through into clear air. Six feet of drift.

A wash of fresh, bitingly cold air blasted down at him mixed with a flurry of snow.

Mick looked up through the six-inch hole he'd punched and saw the blizzard ripping by above them. The wind had little to roar against on a flat surface of powdered snow, so it passed by relatively quietly...and very fast. It would be deafening as soon as they climbed out onto the surface of the snow. It was daylight, but barely.

He ducked back into the tent and saw Patty sitting unmoving in the darkness.

"It'll be okay."

"Duh!" She shook off or buried whatever nerves he'd seen on her face for that brief instant. "We're Special Ops," and in that moment she was.

He squeezed her arm to let her know how much he appreciated her ability to adapt to a changing situation. It was pretty damned impressive even by Night Stalker standards.

"Some things they don't prepare you for so well," she said softly but began cinching up the closures on her hood and prepping to enter the blizzard. So, she didn't have nerves of steel, she just knew how to act as if they were—which had the same result but made her all the more impressive.

Personally, he'd rather stay in their little cocoon than go out in that weather.

"Caspar," he keyed the radio, "this is Mick. Have you punched out yet?"

"Yeah, ugly as ghost slime out there."

"Are we safe to move?"

"Have to," he answered. "And not just because our 'survivor' won't last another night on the mountain. Reports say that this storm gets way worse before it gets better and there's another front behind it. Three days minimum. See you in five minutes."

"Roger that."

" 'Roger that'?" Patty snarked at him. "We're leaving our warm and cozy love nest to crawl into a storm from hell and 'Roger that' is the best you've got?"

Mick keyed the radio, "Patty says that's a 'no go' until after you deliver her hot chocolate, a three-egg omelette with hash browns, and an English muffin with blueberry jam."

She sputtered at him.

"I lost the draw," Caspar replied. "I had to eat the penne with those vegetable sausage crumbles. No sympathy from this tent."

"Sorry, Boston," Mick told her.

"Strawberry jam, Doofus," she shot him one of those radiant but smarmy smiles. "Then apricot and after that blueberry. Certain things you need to know about me if you're going to go on bedding me."

As he definitely planned to go on doing that, he committed the information to memory. It was easy to do as her tastes alternated right down the color spectrum: red, skip orange, yellow, skip green, blue, skip indigo, then violet?

"Bet you hated grape juice as a kid."

"But I loved cranberry and apple. You broke my color code, which is better than my parents ever did." Her grin was wicked, then she went serious. "You lead. I'll collapse the tent behind us."

Even though he'd never met them, he could feel pity for parents with such a precocious child. He crawled back out and worked on building tall steps that would get them out to the surface. Mick hoped that it was just a local drift, because if they had to battle six feet of fresh snow the whole way down the mountain, they were in trouble.

Jostling close enough together to evoke memories of last night's hot sweaty moments, they collapsed the tent in the hole it had kept open in the snow, folded it well enough that it wouldn't cause them trouble during the descent and tied it onto his pack.

Ice axes out and crampons on, they roped up with the PJs and the two toboggans. One the descent, the PJs didn't stop for training lessons, which made the key lesson most obvious: do whatever it takes to get out alive.

They took turns battering a channel through the snow. When Patty had volunteered to take a turn, Caspar had gently blocked her.

"You're too narrow, Patty. We need a path wide enough for us to fit through as well."

Mick appreciated how tactfully the man had done it, Patty was out near her limits—not that it stopped her.

She'd passed the same trials he had. They trained Special Operations soldiers for mental stamina far beyond the physical, because it was when the body gave up that the true soldiering began. Patty didn't back down for a moment; "quit" had been knocked out of her vocabulary as long ago as it had been knocked out of his own.

It was a grueling six hours. Finally they reached the second team and the snow was down to three feet of powder. The second team had spent the morning fighting a trail upward and the storm had only partially refilled it.

They should have picked up speed at that point, but all it did was keep them from losing speed.

At the line where blinding snow shifted to driving rain from above and chilling slush to freezing mud beneath their feet, the third team relieved them of their burdens. They all headed down the mountain together.

The “survivor” made it down alive, but even the PJs were dragging.

And Mick figured that if he was allowed to sleep for about a week, he’d have made it down alive as well.

Patty was still grimly matching him step for step when they were finally retrieved in the flatlands. An Army bus awaited them for the six-hour drive back to Anchorage. They were whipped hard the whole way as they drove deeper into the storm; rain drummed so hard on the metal roof that it was impossible to talk even if he’d had the energy to try. He was damn glad to be off that mountain.

When Patty collapsed against his shoulder, she was asleep before she got there. It didn’t keep him awake for more than a few seconds. But those few were enough to register just how happy he was that she was there.

It was also long enough to wonder at how much his life had changed in the last thirty-six hours. But he was out before he had any time to think about it.

# # #

“Got an opening here for you anytime you want,” Casper and Two-ton had shaken her hand and Mick’s. “That was some damn fine work,” they told Major Napier and strode off as if she and Mick had done no more than win a quick game of racquetball.

Patty didn’t really remember much else about her triumphant return to Joint Base Elmendorf-Richardson. Partly because it was just the end of another training exercise to the Two-Twelve, so no one made any big deal of it.

She also didn't remember it because she couldn't stop falling asleep. She'd given everything she had, and then more, on the mountain as they'd wrestled the toboggans down off the snowy peak. She'd refused to become another victim that would burden her team on the final descent. By the time they were out of the danger zone she knew far too well what it took to wrestle those two heavy "victims" and she wasn't going to become the third.

She'd been led to turn in her gear to the quartermaster, but slept through any chance to rib him about his selection of MREs. One moment she'd been still loaded up in heavy gear and the next she'd been sitting in the Mess Hall and mechanically eating a meal she didn't recall and the next walking along the hallway of the transient lodging hotel.

And now she was in the dark.

The glowing red clock that read 7:30 didn't tell her a thing. First off, what idiot put a civilian clock in a military transient lodging? Heavy curtains would have required her to crawl out of a very warm and comfortable bed to see if it was morning or night. Actually either 7:30 would be dark now, a.m. or p.m. Second, she might have slept an hour or a day. But third, since she didn't know when she'd finally been allowed to crash, it was all worse than meaningless. The clock only pretended to have useful information, but it was obviously lying.

Then there was a very small sound that provided an immense amount of information, a soft sigh. She might be in bed, but she wasn't alone.

Next level of awareness: beneath the covers she was wearing a t-shirt that swam on her, she could practically slither out the neck hole and the sleeves reached her elbows. And she was wearing nothing else.

"You'd better be Mick Quinn," she whispered at the form, but received no answer.

She reached out into the dark and found a shoulder. Mick's? Muscled enough to be.

Then its owner, from lying flat on his back, scooped her against him so that she landed with her head on his shoulder and his arm cradled down her back.

Definitely Mick. It was exactly the position they'd slept in up on Mount Hayes and he felt exactly this way. He smelled so gloriously warm and male there beneath the covers.

But he took no further action.

With another sigh, he was back asleep.

Whatever had passed between them—that they certainly hadn't discussed any further during the brutal mountain descent close beside the two PJs—The Mighty Quinn's subconscious obviously approved of it.

The simple move had also awoken every overstrained muscle fiber in her arms and legs. First it was a twitch, then a spasm, then the hand that was lying so comfortably on Mick's broad chest spasmed hard enough that she clipped him in the chin.

After a surprised grunt and a curse, his hands that had been completely lax clamped onto her.

"Easy," he whispered rather than asking *what the hell?* "Easy. It will pass."

In moments her body bucked and writhed with cramps and charley horses. Mick simply held her and let her flail. Eventually the spasms eased and the sharp pains faded back to mere twitches, then thankful calm.

"I salted your food fairly heavily, but you were too tired to eat much of it or drink any Gatorade."

Patty lay still, afraid to speak or even take a deep breath for fear that the shooting pains would start all over again.

"You sweat out a lot of salt and electrolytes at altitude without noticing. We were working hard up on that mountain. And you built up enough lactic acid for a lifetime. I almost punched out Napier when we got down. He should never have pushed us so hard."

"Punching out a superior officer is frowned on in most circles."

"Yeah," he chuckled softly, "especially when that officer is Pete Napier. The only thing that saved me from having my ass kicked and thrown into the brig was Danielle got one good look at you and went after him for me."

"Go, Danielle."

"Yeah. There was something strange though. Napier never does anything by accident. He whispered something to Danielle and she backed right down. Didn't look any less angry, but something else was going on."

Patty felt a sudden chill and snuggled tighter against Mick's warmth as he stroked a hand idly up and down her back.

"Something else…" he tested the words as he spoke them.

"What? Like a new mission?"

"Maybe," she could feel Mick's nod. "Yeah, more than maybe. He wanted us, you and me, to parachute in. Work with the PJs. He specifically wanted us to get that ice-and-snow training."

"No. That wasn't him, we volunteered. You volunteered us." But even as she said it, she knew. "And if someone else had volunteered…"

"Napier would have switched us into their places with a simple, 'Why don't we let Mick and Patty take this one?' Nobody would gainsay him."

"Gainsay. Pretty fancy word for an Alaska fisheryboy."

"Sass. Pretty standard from Patty O'Donoghue."

Since there was no point in arguing that, she concentrated on something else…like how good Mick smelled. Whereas, "I smell like something the polar bear dragged in."

"Better than something the penguin barfed up," he made a point of sniffing her hair. "But not by much."

"Why don't you smell like that?"

"Because I showered. If I tried to shower you last night, I was afraid you would drown, so I just held my nose and stuffed you between the sheets."

Patty sniffed at herself again. "Ick! Real attractive. I gotta shower. Don't go anywhere. I'll make it worth your while."

"Deal."

By the time she was at least sanitary if not fully decontaminated, Mick was fast asleep again. It had been so much fun waking him the first time, she couldn't wait to do it again.

She slipped in between the covers and snuggled up to him. He was out, not even curling his arm around her. She reached down to—

A hard pounding on the door was followed by Napier calling out.

"Up, Quinn. Enough beauty sleep."

"Goddamn it," Patty kept her voice soft because she certainly didn't want the major to know where she'd spent the night. That would not go down well at all. She and Mick in bed together definitely warranted a disciplinary action, if not something far more serious.

"You too, Boston!" Napier beat the door once more before his footsteps tromped off down the hall and he began battering down the next door.

"*Goddamn it!*" She didn't bother to keep her voice down on that one.

Napier might have chuckled as he moved down the hall.

Now what the hell had that meant?

Chapter 6

The time was 2000 hours when Major Napier had rousted the team. By 2030 they had breakfasted and assembled in the hangar, all staring at their aircraft in bewilderment. Well, everyone except Napier who looked slightly smug, and the two mechanics, Connie and Big John, who looked harried.

None of the changes were explained which was making Mick feel more than a little grumpy. He hoped that was rooted in lack of sleep and not lack of sex with Patty, because no way could he allow his personal life into his military one.

Napier hadn't pulled him aside; hadn't made a single sign. Mick was a Lieutenant sleeping with a Chief Warrant Officer, even if all they'd done last night was sleep. At least Patty wasn't an enlisted—not anymore—but it still wasn't right. Yet, Napier hadn't said a word. So still no change there.

It was his helo that was changed.

The *Linda's* two outer weapons' hard points had been replaced by long-range fuel tanks. The weapons that now hung from the inner hard points on his Little Bird were no longer American.

They were Russian.

They'd been repainted, but it wasn't going to fool anyone. The Ugroza missile pod had replaced his Hydra 70s and the Yak-B Gatling gun had supplanted the M134 minigun.

The weapons were absolutely not certified to be on his bird. Their weight and capability were similar enough to what had been removed that it shouldn't be a problem, but he couldn't make sense of the change. Any idiot who looked at those weapons wasn't going to be fooled by the American stealth helicopter attached to them.

Patty shook her head at him sadly from where she knelt inspecting the attachment points, "You always were the slow one on our team, Quinn."

"Me? I didn't say a word."

"Didn't need to. It's all *ov-ah* that pretty face of yours *yawz*," she laid on an extra thick helping of her accent.

He rubbed his eyes. He felt rested; he was never the slow one. But just being around Patty it sounded like he was sometimes… it sounded.

Oh! That was the key.

"The sleeping bear awakens," Patty snorted.

He placed a hand on the top of her head and pressed down. She went from squat to sprawl with a very satisfying thump and a quite descriptive curse.

"My moth-*ah*," he imitated her, "has never said that she'd wished she'd gotten a dog instead of me for a son."

"Didn't need to," she answered from the concrete floor. "Some things are just that obvious."

He ignored her self-satisfied grin. It was the *sound* that mattered. At night, in the dark, no one would see their Little Bird, not even most radar equipment. But if they had to fire weapons, they couldn't sound American or fire American rounds.

A quick scan showed similar changes on all of the other aircraft. The *Beatrix,* being a heavier DAP Hawk, now sported a Shipunov 2A42 30mm cannon, which Rafe, Julian, and their gunner Drake, were inspecting with admiration on their faces. The cannon was a nasty-looking piece of hardware even if most of it was tucked inside a composite, radar-absorbent housing.

Stealth American helicopters with Russian armament.

The Chinook was little changed. The crew chiefs' three M134 Gatling guns had been replaced and a massive fuel bladder of four thousand gallons of JP-5 jet fuel now filled the main cargo bay. Add that to the extended-range fuel tanks on *Linda* and *Leeloo*. They were going a long way from any friendly filling station. All the way to—

"Oh man," Patty connected the pieces at the same moment he did and grimaced.

He held out a hand and helped her to her feet.

Napier was down at the far end of the hangar by the Avenger drone with Sofia, her copilot, and a woman with long dark hair that he didn't recognize. When they were all done marveling at the changes to their own aircraft, they gathered around them.

Instead of one Avenger drone parked at the far end of the hangar, Sofia's *Raven*—named for Marion Ravenwood in *Indiana Jones*—had grown a twin. As far as Mick knew, only three had ever been built. To have two of them here told him just how hairy this mission might get.

"These," Major Napier rested a hand on one of the drone's blunt noses, "will be forward deployed to Eareckson Air Station on Shemya Island near the end of the Aleutians along with a refueling and maintenance team from the Pac Air Force Regional Support who will *not* be told our mission."

"Not like we've been told squat either!"

Mick laughed at Patty's snide remark. It was the perfect tension breaker. It was definitely frustrating to be heading aloft with no information other than they were flying into Russia. But he wouldn't have dared to drop that in the major's lap. Patty shrugged at him as if to say, *No guts, no glory!*

Napier waited out the laugh before continuing as if nothing had happened. "Sofia and Zoe, you will control the flights from your coffin here. We've also borrowed Captain Kara Moretti from the 5D," Napier introduced the sultry woman with Mediterranean skin and a sparkling wedding ring, "to trade off shifts with you. The *Rita* is her aircraft."

"Hayworth?" Patty guessed.

Moretti shook her head in a swirl of dark hair. Her smile was sassy and reminded him of Patty even though their coloring had nothing in common.

"Rita Moreno from *West Side Story?*" was Julian's shot at it and others began tossing out ideas.

"MacDowell in *Groundhog Day?*"

"Nah. Though Andie was hot in that."

Mick knew who it was. It hadn't been hard to figure out that all of their aircraft were named for exceptional action heroines, though that trick of Danielle's had avoided her husband's notice until it was too late.

"*Edge of Tomorrow,*" he spoke up and Moretti tapped her finger on the tip of her nose. "Rita was the ultimate warrior. Emily Blunt with Tom Cruise defeating the alien, time-warping scourge across Europe. She, to use Patty's term, totally kicked ass." Since that movie, Ms. Blunt had moved way high on his gotta-meet-that-woman-someday list. Though the other idle fantasies that had gone along with that no longer seemed to matter with Patty looking at him with that goofy grin of hers as if she knew exactly what he was thinking.

Napier scowled at Danielle for a moment then simply sighed before continuing. "Eareckson is an hour from our destination and the Avenger remotes have a flight duration of eighteen hours. We expect you to keep an eye in the air above us at all times. Stay out of sight but we may need your craft's eyes and ears."

Sofia looked relieved at being left to work from somewhere warmer than the icy slopes of Mount Hayes. Mick had checked in with her on the descent and she'd done better than he expected. She actually understood and integrated their one talk in the Mess

Hall straight into the harsh realities in the field. Completely deserved to be in Special Operations.

"Airborne in ten. Let's go!" Napier clapped his gloved hands together and they all hurried to prepare their aircraft.

He and Patty did their preflight in silence, got their engines started, and waited while someone doused the hangar's lights before sliding open the big doors.

By 2100 hours, just an hour after he'd woken up in bed with Patty still beside him, he scooted the *Linda* forward out of the hangar and pulled aloft.

He'd actually expected her to discretely slip off after her shower. Not that he expected her to cover for them, rather that he figured that she would prefer less connection between them.

Mick had taken her into his bed in the first place because he wasn't about to feel her up in the hallway to find where she'd stashed her own room's keycard and because she was so exhausted he'd been half worried that she'd stop breathing. That she'd returned to his bed after her shower had surprised him no end.

It had also pleased him.

Rather than avoiding him after what they'd done in the mountain tent, she had chosen to curl back up against him. If a beautiful woman wanted to be in his bed, his ego wasn't going to complain for a second.

If Patty O'Donoghue wanted to be there, he'd count himself a very lucky man.

And that was the most surprising thought of them all.

# # #

Ten hours and two refueling stops later, Patty groaned dramatically going for the laugh.

She didn't get the response, but that didn't worry her. If he was half has tired and stiff as she was from spending so long in the tiny cockpit, then he wouldn't have the energy for a laugh.

Besides, Mick was busy fighting the controls to bring the Little Bird shimmying down out of the dull gray sky. Not a storm front this time, just rotten weather and too damn long in the air.

"The Aleutians. Again," she said with disgust. "Personally I felt that one visit was plenty for this island chain."

"Look at the bright side. We didn't even get to see the islands last time; it was all a night flight."

"You're right, Mick. As usual. Because this," she waved a hand toward the front windscreen, "is so much better."

Desolate didn't begin to describe Attu Island. They were almost a thousand miles past where they'd been harassing the KPN fleet a few days ago. Attu lay several islands and half a hundred miles farther west than even Eareckson Air Station, where the Avenger drones had been staged. And the breaking dawn light wasn't making it any more attractive.

"You know," Patty twisted in her seat once more. "After ten hours cramped up in a Little Bird seat, downtown Paris wouldn't look attractive."

"I bet they have hotels there. Nice ones."

"Probably," she'd never been Paris, only to Pau to train with their 4th Special Forces Helicopter Regiment.

"We could go."

"I think we have something else we're supposed to be doing right now."

Mick didn't respond.

Had she just turned down a romantic vacation in Paris with Mick Quinn? Uh…maybe. Well, that was stupid by any woman's standards.

Mick had them down close by the shore and Patty guided him toward the southeastern cove on the island. Apparently he wasn't going to be the one to speak next.

"That sounds wonderful, Quinn." Oh man, did it ever.

"It's a date," he said it like he was going to take her out for pizza.

Something had slipped by her but she was so tired that she was having trouble pinning it down. Making a date to be with

Mick in Paris felt…normal. Which it wasn't. Or was it? Not thinking clearly, she gave it up for the moment.

She felt battered, even more than she had by the storm on Mount Hayes. A Little Bird was designed for the quick tactical strike, not for a ten-hour long ferrying flight from Anchorage to the westernmost Aleutian Island that was still part of the United States. In fact it was so far west that it was east—on the other side of the International Dateline. Only one other island kept it from being the easternmost point of the United States as well as the westernmost of Alaska.

Attu was a lumpy rock fifty miles long and twenty wide. Mostly snow-capped peaks cragging up to three thousand feet. Only one valley was any more than a dent in the mountains and it was barely longer than the old Coast Guard runway that filled it from one end to the other.

Amend that, *abandoned* Coast Guard runway.

Not a single tree showed on the whole island. Just valleys of snarled grasses and a whole lot of steep rock and ice. Patty saw no reason to amend her initial assessment that once was two times too many.

When the four helos got their skids and wheels down, Patty hit the radio transmit switch. She flipped to the low power antenna, so the signal wouldn't travel much outside their immediate group.

"Greetings, campers. We have just increased this island's population by thirteen people and four helicopters. In case you were wondering, that brings the island's population to…wait for it…a grand freaking total of—"

"—thirteen people and four helicopters." Mick echoed her voice. Even his wry tone and accent matched hers.

"Always been a lucky number for me," Mick remarked off air.

"That's because you're a loon."

"I'm not from Minnesota or Ontario."

"Whatever," she was too sore and weary to argue.

"Loons are the state bird of one and the provincial bird of the other."

Patty laughed and Mick smiled along with her but probably for different reasons. Mick was loosening up, making second-level jokes like that. He was so cute.

Patty had gone through very mixed feelings on the long flight from Anchorage. Initial frustration that their wake-up sex had been interrupted before it began. She'd really wanted to see if what had occurred between them on the mountain had been strictly environmental, or if Quinn was really that spectacular a lover. Having a king-size bed and no opportunity to test the possible results had wound her up and crashed her down.

It was only after they were airborne that Napier's steadfast silence on the topic of Mick and her being in the same bed began to worry her. It was fine. Well, not really, but at least mostly okay that Napier and Danielle were together—they were captain and major after all even if they were in the same damned unit. And Connie Davis and John Wallace were both sergeants. Besides, they'd arrived married. Some prior commander had seen fit to allow it and still let them serve together.

But she was enlisted and Mick was a Lieutenant. Okay, she was a Chief Warrant 3, a commissioned officer like Mick, but not like Mick. They certainly shouldn't be fraternizing, even if they were. Had been. Once.

Maybe the 5th Battalion E Company was *extreme* in more ways than their equipment and their missions. Were they some kind of command-sanctioned coed experiment? She didn't like that thought anymore than the rest of them.

Patty had spent the next part of the flight feeling very grumpy about being a lab rat in any incarnation: past, present, or future. And then she'd decided that the answer might be much simpler. The 5E was so clandestine an outfit, that few people outside the unit knew they existed. Well, other than the 5D whose butts they'd whupped (kinda) during training.

Maybe it was just a tolerant commander who wouldn't bust her ass as long as she performed absolutely perfectly at every instant.

Having reached that conclusion, her body decided to make another effort to catch up on the physical abuse from the mountain rescue. She'd passed out for the last three hours of the flight, something Patty would have to apologize to Mick for later. She hadn't even known it was physically possible to sleep in a pilot's seat in the Little Bird.

Looking out the windscreen made her wish she was still off in some pleasant dreamland.

On Attu Island, all color had been washed away. There was white snow, dark rock, brown grass with early snow trapped around its roots. A low gray sky and thin mist darkened everything even further.

The only thing that broke the wasteland was the concrete structure and radio tower of the old US Coast Guard LORAN station for guiding ships and planes. Nobody needed LORAN anymore to navigate, not with GPS satellites whirling overhead. In the half dozen years since the Coast Guard had declared good riddance and took off, the Bering Sea winters had battered the old station.

The U-shaped two-story building showed the wear and tear of Arctic storms battering the facade. It too was plain white and added no color to the landscape. The small windows were still intact, but the paint was peeling.

"What a place we've come to."

"Beyond here there be dragons," Mick agreed.

"Did you just make a joke? Mick Quinn. Really?"

"Eat shit, O'Donoghue."

There was another first. She wasn't sure that Mick had ever cursed at her before—she had the foul mouth of this team. Patty decided that she'd take it as a compliment that he'd unwound enough to do so.

Instead, she did what all of the rest of the Night Stalkers were doing, she climbed out of the helo, moving like some billion-year-old biddy.

"I'm like an *Australopithecus* after a hard day foraging in the wilderness that would someday be named Africa."

"You're too tall and nowhere near hairy enough. Which I appreciate."

"You say the sweetest things, Quinn."

"You sure are stooped over like one, though."

If she'd had the energy to circle around the helo, she'd have bludgeoned him with a stone. She didn't.

Instead she helped him secure the bird, covering the more sensitive equipment, slipping tie-down sleeves on the rotor blades so they wouldn't whirl with the wind.

The northerly winds were blockaded from the runway by a ridgeline of tall peaks, but still the bitter fog swirled close about them as she pulled on her cold weather gear.

They pulled visual tarps over the aircraft, so that if someone happened to fly by, extremely unlikely, they wouldn't notice the stealth nature of the helos. The secret that the Night Stalkers were actively fielding stealth rotorcraft wouldn't last forever, but they'd hold off the inevitable as long as possible.

Even as Patty thought that, a Pave Hawk—the Air Force's version of the Sikorsky Black Hawk—came roaring down out of the sullen sky. It landed clean and very close beside them.

She glanced at Mick, but he shook his head. He didn't know what they were doing here either.

As soon as the back ramp was down, a refueling team began running hoses from the Pave Hawk's cargo bay over to the 5E's helos. Their own crew still hadn't touched the large fuel bladder lying in the back of the *Carrie-Anne* Chinook helo. It was clear to see that the refueling crews had been ordered to display no curiosity at all. They barely lifted their heads enough to find where to attach their fuel hoses.

Then two more men came trooping off the Pave Hawk, except one was a woman.

But there was no mistaking what they were or that it meant the 5E was in for a world of hurt.

Chapter 7

SEAL Commander Luke Altman had them assemble in the USCG LORAN station's rec room as soon as the Pave Hawk was back aloft.

"Lousy service," Patty whispered in Mick's ear.

He had to agree. The old station was cold and even though the room was oddly intact, it felt truly abandoned. White walls, linoleum floor, four-person Formica tables and rust-pitted-chrome and plastic chairs. Motivational slogans were peeling off one wall, and the bar—with its sign announcing a four-beer limit per person per night—no longer stocked beer, soda, or snacks.

Somewhere a generator groaned to life and the lights over the bar wavered on. Connie and Big John came wandering in.

"The fuel is old and thick," John announced. "But it still fires off. They didn't leave much in the tanks. We'll have lights and some heat in this room and we're pumping heat into the barracks for at least the next few hours. We'll go to bed warm, but probably wake up cold."

Mick and Patty shoved tables together in the still-frozen air, everyone's breath showed in white vaporous clouds, but he could already feel a wash of warm air from the ceiling vents.

"Great service," Mick whispered back to Patty.

"Still no cold beer."

"If there was, it would be frozen and we wouldn't be allowed to have a drink anyway."

"Nitpicker. Besides, that's not the point."

"Then what is the point?" Someday he'd figure out Patty's sense of humor, but he actually sort of hoped not. He liked that she kept surprising him.

"That I can't have a beer even if I wanted to break the rules. Seems awfully stingy. As if the Coast Guard knew we were coming and didn't leave any behind on purpose."

"Do you take *everything* personally?"

"Absolutely!"

They dragged fifteen chairs into place around the square arrangement of tables. Patty dragged over an extra, dropped into a corner seat and then stretched out her legs on the extra chair.

How could such a simple gesture send his thoughts churning off into such drastically veering directions? Mick remembered the feel of those legs wrapped around him. He remembered how smooth and perfect they'd looked when he'd slipped her into bed last night, a soldier's legs. A woman's.

He headed for a chair across from her and then caught himself. Was he trying to avoid sitting next to her because it would be inappropriate? Or was he wanting to sit far enough away that he could watch her?

Patty's scowl warned him that he was on the verge of being drastically rude for not sitting next to her. Duh! So he changed course, but it was too late. Connie and then Big John sat to one side of her. Danielle sat to the other.

By the time he got his feet in motion, the only spot remaining was between Danielle and the Team 6 Commander. Luke Altman was bigger than everyone except Big John. The SEAL was six-four of warrior who made even Mick feel a little small and humbled.

His silent fellow SEAL, Specialist Nikita Hayward—though no one was saying specialist in what other than warfare, which was a given if she'd made it into Team 6—had plugged a tiny projector into a tablet computer and aimed it at a white wall. Nikita was almost as daunting as her commander. Just under six feet tall and strong enough to have survived the Team 6 testing, she stood out completely even in this crowd.

Night Stalkers needed to be both fit and skilled; Nikita was Amazonian. Her dark hair was layer cut and framed an open face. But it was her dark eyes that were that were her knock-out feature. She looked at everyone with a simple frankness that missed absolutely nothing.

Several of the guys squirmed a little beneath her unblinking gaze. Jason, the *Carrie-Anne's* ramp gunner, just stared like he couldn't help himself.

"This," Altman signaled to Nikita for the first slide, "is the Kamchatka Peninsula. The easternmost land of Russia except for a few stray islands even sadder than the one we're sitting on right here. Almost entirely separated from the mainland by the Sea of Okhotsk, it's a five-hundred mile ocean crossing from here. The size of California, it includes: almost two hundred volcanoes with thirty active ones, massive populations of salmon and grizzly bears, and already it's wrapped in snow and ice down to a thousand feet of elevation. The entire area has a population one third the size of San Francisco and most live in the peninsula's single city, Petropavlovsk-Kamchatsky, also known as PK."

"That makes for a whole lot of nothing," Patty observed and received a nod from the Team 6 commander.

"Uh-huh," Altman agreed and Specialist Nikita flicked to the next slide.

The reactions around the table were varied.

To Mick it looked like another drone.

Several people, including Patty flinched.

"Shit!" She scanned the table and then slapped her forehead. "Right, they aren't here. Sofia would freak if she saw this."

"She has seen this photo and your assessment is correct," Nikita offered a rare comment. "I showed this information to Lieutenant Gracie and Specialist Zoe DeMille, her copilot. Lieutenant Gracie's reaction was 'That! It does no exist!'" It was a better than fair imitation of Sofia's accent when she grew excited. "She then went on at length in Portuguese, which I don't speak, but she seemed quite upset."

One drone looked a lot like the next to Mick. They mostly fell into three categories: cute little ones with tiny propellers, big nasty ones like the Predator and Sofia's Avenger, and the flying wing things. The last looked like small versions of the F-117 Nighthawk fighter and B-2 Spirit bomber. Like someone mounted a cockpit and a big damn engine onto the middle of a giant black boomerang. Whatever this drone was, it fell into the third category. It was a flying wing thing with a Russian Sukhoi Su-30 fighter jet in formation close alongside. The image looked like an advertising shot—magazine slick.

He scanned the table. Connie was fascinated, others were perplexed, and Patty, the sneak, was shaking her head at him once more.

"Uh," Mick figured he'd take the hit, "can someone explain that thing to me."

"Better make it in small words," Patty teased.

"Sofia was quite right," Commander Altman waved a hand at the screen. "It doesn't exist. According to the best reports we have it shouldn't have its first flight for three more years, or be operational for five."

"Could that be Photoshop?" It was a blue sky photo. The drone looked as if it had been cut right into the photo with its oddly angled lines.

"I've been assured that this is not a staged photo or Photoshop; it's flying now."

Patty collapsed back in her seat as Altman continued his lecture.

"Lieutenant Gracie's Avenger is an RPA and she controls it, occasionally allowing its autopilot to control long ferries or the fussy details of a takeoff or landing. Because it can carry armament, it could be better classed as a UCAV, an Unmanned Combat Aerial Vehicle. But if this Russian UCAV is like our own X-47 tests, it has an extremely low-observable profile and can be programmed to operate autonomously. We've had ours land itself on an aircraft carrier multiple times. In theory, you could tell one of these to fly thousands of miles and drop a nuke at a pre-programmed target and the bomb would have a bigger radar signature while falling than the aircraft that's carrying it."

"Holy shit!" Patty's soft curse was echoed around the table.

It summed up Mick's feelings completely.

"According to everything we've heard from the primary drone labs near Moscow, this is barely off the drawing boards and not expected to be a threat for another five years. This picture is from a previously unknown development base in Kamchatka. We've been asked to fly over and check it out."

No one was able to laugh, not when faced with Commander Altman's deadpan delivery.

And by the silence, Mick guessed that he wasn't the only one stunned past swearing.

# # #

Patty didn't care what anyone thought or said, she took her sleeping bag, found Mick's room by using her flashlight—the shuttered windows kept out the thin, gray daylight—and joined him in the darkness on his narrow bunk.

They didn't zip their bags together.

He simply shuffled back against the wall. She lay her bag down beside him, crawled inside and buried her face against his chest. He stroked her hair and kissed her atop the head.

"Where does this go, Mick?"

"Definitely Kamchatka," he gave her one of his naive answers.

"No, I…" Then she remembered that no matter what he might show the world to keep them at ease, he was anything but naive. "Sorry, my 'goofy meter' isn't functioning very well at the moment. It's also not calibrated to you."

"Doesn't matter, Gloucester," he whispered into her hair. He didn't even tease her with his usual "Glaow-chester" mispronunciation; giving her the proper "Glaw-stuh" instead.

"That's better than 'Boston' anyway."

"I was going to come find you, but…" he trailed off.

"It would have besmirched your stoic manliness to be afraid of the dark, especially because it's the middle of the day."

"Something like that."

She liked that she could feel his smile where his lips still pressed atop her head. She snuggled in tighter, felt safe for the first time since the briefing. Well, safer.

"It's easier if you can believe that we're the technologically superior force."

Patty just kept her face buried against his chest and let the words buzz through his breastbone and the bridge of her nose where it tickled a little.

"We cooked up the bomb, even defeated Germany before they could cook up one of their own. Gave us an edge for a while. Once we figured out rockets, we dusted everybody: the moon and all that. We even got the International Space Station. Everyone knows it's mostly ours, we even paid for or built most of the Russian components because they couldn't afford to. We have stealth and UAVs cornered…until suddenly we don't."

"It's not fair." She didn't want the world to change faster than she was ready for. "I joined to get away from the danger."

Mick's snort of laughter warmed the top of her head. "You went Special Operations to get *away* from danger? Christ, only Patty O'Donoghue would do something like that."

"No, Doofus. I went National Guard to get away from watching my brother lose his leg to a shark that came up in the seine net. To not watch my brother-in-law get caught in a rogue wave that washed over the boat and widow my sister when his hold slipped. In the Guard, helo pilots pluck people out of floods and fly training missions. My tours in the dustbowl were brief and…"

"And?" Mick's soft murmur encouraged her.

"And I was bored as shit. I applied for Night Stalkers on a dare."

"That's my Patty."

She wasn't his anything…even if she did like the way it sounded. She'd never actually admitted all this to anyone, but it felt safe, almost important, to tell Mick.

"So why did you stick with it?"

"My reputation," it sounded stupid when she said it that way, but it was true.

"Explain that."

"My reputation caught up with me. You know, all those things you learn on a fishing boat. Safety first, be level-headed in a crisis, hard work is better than the empty net of a waterhaul because it means your family will get to eat that winter. All that crap."

Mick kissed her hair. "Yeah, I know 'all that crap' too."

"Well, my commanders kept recommending me upward. Then the Night Stalkers hooked me with promises that I'd be the best." At the moment she felt like shit. All the underpinnings of her world were crumbling. The Russians were scaling up for another cold war. And they were building *and flying* stealth UCAVs.

She was such a mess. It even bothered her that she was the one who'd been afraid of the "dark" and come running to her lover's arms. Did once even count as "lover"? She wasn't supposed to be curled up in some guy's arms seeking solace, not even if they were Mick's.

"Why did you join?" She could feel the change in him the moment she asked.

While they'd been talking, Mick's hold on her had eased off. Not that he'd moved, he'd just been holding her less hard. Now he pulled her back in tightly enough that she had to turn her head to the side if she didn't want her nose squished against his breastbone.

"It's okay, honey." She wanted to brush a hand down his back, tell him it would be okay and he didn't have to say anything. But her arms were trapped inside her sleeping bag up against her chest.

He took a short, sharp breath. Then a deep, longer one that almost squished her because he didn't ease off on his hold of her at all.

Unable to do anything, all she could do was wait.

He finally blew out the breath in a loud whoosh.

"We lost a boat. Our family lost a boat."

"Oh shit!" Her family had never lost a boat, but Gloucester as a community lost a boat every couple years. And when you lost a boat in the North Atlantic, you usually lost the crew too. It gutted the community. Just because the movie *The Perfect Storm* told the tale of the *Andrea Gail,* didn't mean the losses had stopped.

"The Coast Guard rescue team," Mick continued, "the peacetime version of the PJs we just trained with, flew out and dropped two swimmers. It was sixty and fifty."

Patty pictured a sixty-knot storm and fifty-foot waves. She'd been out working on a boat in that kind of weather a few times and it was sure as hell why she flew in warm and dry helicopters for a living.

"The two of them saved all eighteen of our people. One at a time, in that serious-as-hell weather."

"Wow." There was nothing else to say, it must have been an amazing feat.

"One of the swimmers didn't make it."

"'That others may live.'" Patty blinked hard against the tears. The swimmers and PJs shared that motto.

Most people, especially those inside the military looked up to the Special Operations soldiers as heroes.

Inside Spec Ops, everyone, absolutely everyone looked up to the PJs. Each time one lost his life it was a blow that could be felt all through the community no matter what branch of the military your team technically belonged to. And a Coast Guard rescue swimmer was right up there with a PJ.

"I tried to go into the water for a career. I washed out, wasn't good enough. Air Force Pararescue has a ninety percent failure rate and I was part of it."

Patty tried to imagine Mick failing at anything he set out to do but couldn't quite manage it.

"Our family's lead boat, the one I was on, arrived just in time for us to watch the rescue swimmer get trapped in the wreckage and be dragged under. I couldn't get past that image during testing and it kept me from making the cut. Figured if I couldn't swim, then I'd deliver the swimmers."

"Helicopters," Patty whispered against his chest.

"Helicopters," Mick agreed.

And in that instant Patty knew that she was totally screwed. It had been hard enough stepping up to Mick's standard every day, even if she was a better woman for it.

But living up to the standard of his love, how was she supposed to do that?

Well, she'd better find a way because she'd just learned that she was sure-as-shit in love with this man.

They didn't speak another word. Not when the generator finally ran out of fuel and the heat shut down. Not when the first chill crept back out of the concrete walls forcing them deeper into their bags.

They curled up tightly against each other through their separate sleeping bags and it was a long time before either of them slept.

Chapter 8

Five hundred miles," Major Napier announced as they gathered, each wearing heavy winter gear around the table in the Attu Island USCG rec room. Mick looked around. They were a tribe of giant snowmen, even the women—but all in non-reflective Night Stalker black.

Pathetic! That was such a Patty-type of bizarre image, and now it was in his head. Mick wondered briefly if she was doing some kind of telepathic thing, showing him quite how strange her view of the world was.

Patty was so layered up it would have been impossible to tell her from Sofia except for the light skin and blue eyes that had tracked his every move. Something was different with her this morning, but Mick couldn't quite put his finger on it.

Maybe she was just cold. Once the generator had run out of the last dregs of fuel, the chill day had worn away at the building's minimal heat reserve. The indoor temperature had fallen to within a few degrees of outdoor ambient—five degrees below freezing. With the onset of evening it was getting colder.

"Five hundred miles and a three hour flight to the next piece of land…and from here on, neither the land nor the sea will be friendly. Sunset is," Napier checked his watch, "right now." He said it as if it was setting to his command rather than Mother Nature's. With Major Napier, you never knew. Just maybe it had.

He handed around rendezvous coordinates, both primary and secondary in case the primary was occupied by Russians. If it was, the secondary had better be clear because the Little Birds would have to land soon either way.

"This is a hard stretch right out at the fuel limits for the Little Birds, but Commander Altman and I have determined that you are highly necessary assets for the operation's success. If you stumble upon an unfriendly asset and are unable to avoid it, you do not have the spare fuel to engage. Keep flying. The *Beatrix* and the *Carrie-Anne* will be sweeping along behind you and we'll deal with the problem. The ocean is calm tonight, at least by Bering Sea standards. Stay low, move fast, do *not* catch a wave." He aimed the last at Kenny, the Little Bird *Leeloo's* copilot, who was an avid surfer.

"Yes, sir," Kenny "Geek" Rumford, a serious electronics whiz in addition to being a California surfer boy, saluted with all the crispness of a parade ground recruit facing his first three-star general. "Too damn cold anyway, Major Napier, sir."

"Wimp!" His pilot, Malcolm "M&M" Manfred, punched him on the arm. "Life expectancy submerged in this shit is at least four or five minutes, Geek. Where's your board? I'll drop you off on the way."

"Left it stuck up your mama's—"

"Airborne in five," Napier cut them off.

In the chill of the lingering twilight, Mick and Patty preflighted the *Linda* and soon everyone was in the air.

Mick wanted to ask Patty what was the change, because her curious look hadn't dropped behind like Attu Island. And it hadn't changed when the warmth from the cabin heater let them at least unzip their heavy parkas.

But now was not the time.

Flying along at five thousand feet from Anchorage to Attu yesterday had been a casual enough operation.

Departing Attu at fifty feet over dark and formless waves was quite another. Fifty feet up at a hundred and fifty miles an hour placed them under half a second from a watery plunge into the depths.

Patty worked the passive listening devices out to their limits. Infrared, radio, active Russian radar that might be searching for intruders. There would be very few cargo vessels in these waters. Russian, Japanese, and American fisherman were probably the only ships that would be here, though they didn't want to run into any of them either. She'd also be monitoring the helo's well-being and—

"This is *Leeloo*. We appear to have an issue."

Mick felt his entire body flinch at the low-power radio transmission—the first break in an hour of silence. Only by careful training did his hands remain still.

"Go ahead," Napier replied

Mick could see the Chinook using its superior power to quickly close the three mile gap they'd been maintaining.

"Negative fuel flow from starboard auxiliary tank. We can't fix it in the air. If I find out it was one of those Air Farce refueling dweebs, I'll—" M&M managed to cut himself off.

Mick glanced at Patty and she gave him a thumbs up. She'd already tested their tanks and they were good.

"Point of no return in fifteen minutes," M&M came back on the air but still sounded pissed beneath his professional calm. Without the fuel in that tank, they'd fall from the sky a hundred miles from the Russian coast. And in fifteen minutes they wouldn't have enough fuel to get back to Attu.

The *Beatrix* and the *Carrie-Anne* had mid-air refueling probes that could be extended out to guzzle several hundred gallons of Jet-A from a friendly tanker. The Little Birds weren't big enough to support that much extra equipment; they had to make the crossing on their own tanks.

Now came the tough call and it didn't take Napier more than a second. Damn but the man was impressive.

"*Leeloo.* Turn immediately for return to Attu Island."

The other Little Bird hesitated for a long moment, than slammed a vicious turn. Mick couldn't imagine how frustrated M&M and Geek were at this moment.

"*Beatrix* you will fly escort for the *Leeloo* only until a Pave Hawk from Shemya can take over from you." Because helicopters, especially broken ones, did not fly alone over vast reaches of freezing waters.

Mick could hear Danielle on the radio in the background. Napier and Danielle made such a seamless team that they might have been a single voice.

"A KC-135 tanker," Napier was relaying the information even as Danielle and Sofia were making it happen, "will meet *Beatrix* for a mid-air refuel and then escort the *Beatrix* back to our group while the Air Force Pave Hawk escorts *Leeloo* back to land. Rafe, your DAP Hawk has a strong speed advantage over our *Linda* and the *Carrie-Anne*, use it on the return. We want to arrive at the Russian coast as a unit."

And without the *Beatrix* for escort, the *Leeloo* would have no way to rejoin them. They had just gone from four aircraft to three for this mission; five to four if he counted Sofia's Avenger even now high above them.

Mick watched the tactical display as *Beatrix* fell in close behind the crippled Little Bird. It was said that a helicopter wasn't an aircraft, it was a million parts flying in close formation. Night Stalkers' operational availability exceeded all other outfits. The Air Force barely managed a seventy-five percent Mission Capable Rate across the hundred different models of aircraft they flew—the big bombers ran closer to fifty. The 160th SOAR held a full investigation into every single failure and managed to maintain an MCR percentage in the high nineties outside of scheduled maintenance, the best in the business. But it could never be a hundred and *Leeloo* had just drawn the short straw.

"Better to have poor fuel flow than a rotor falling off," Patty commented over the intercom.

Mick laughed a little, "Leave it to you to find the bright side, Gloucester."

"I'm just a bright-side kinda girl."

"Thought you were a woman."

She made a raspberry sound over the intercom loud enough that it echoed inside his helmet.

Mick kept pushing west. A hundred and fifty miles down, three hundred to go.

"I suddenly feel kinda naked out here," her voice barely a whisper this time.

"I've seen you naked. That's a very good thing." But Mick knew exactly what she meant. He kept glancing down at the tactical display and there was only the one other blip—Danielle's big Chinook, the *Carrie-Anne,* still hanging three miles back. It was a lot of empty ocean. Rolling waves that he couldn't see and shining stars that had slipped out unnoticed some time after they escaped Attu.

"A very good thing right back at you, Quinn."

And it was the first time her voice had sounded normal since they'd woken up this morning.

\# # #

Patty was still trying to make sense of what had happened. She and Mick had made love once, well, twice but in the same night and morning up on Mount Hayes. And that had been less than forty-eight hours ago.

She'd never gone soft in the head for any man, if she didn't count a multi-year teenage crush on *The Foo Fighters* drummer Taylor Hawkins. A crush she wasn't entirely sure she was over at thirty.

Plenty of men came to her for comfort; it's what men thought women were for. But it wasn't something Patty ever did in turn. One of Patty's very first memories was being afraid of the thunder and her father's cheery jibe of, "You gotta get your shit together, kid!"

She'd made a career out of having her shit together.

Being around Mick Quinn made her feel both worse and better. Worse that she'd gone to him seeking solace and better for having found it.

Now she rode her hands on their connected flight controls and could echo the immense skill that simply flowed from Mick. The connection was deep, not just through the controls, but also uncomfortable places that were near the heart she'd never really believed she had. Books and other women described such things, but it wasn't anything she believed in.

"I can take it if you need a break."

"You have control," Mick agreed. And just that easily she was Pilot in Command.

"After two years of flying with you, Quinn, you think I'd be used to being trusted." Patty paid careful attention to her flight level. Normally she'd see if she could fly a few feet lower than Mick had been—shave that edge just a little. Not this time. She even let herself float up another five feet so that she could concentrate a bit more on the bigger picture.

"Trust is a big issue for you, Gloucester?"

"At times." And lately, the challenge of entirely trusting herself, which she was *not* going to voice aloud. She had experience with men, but not with what she was feeling about this particular man. This was territory as foreign as the fast-approaching Kamchatka Peninsula.

Chapter 9

Kamchatka Peninsula," Mick said as they slid along with their skids a dozen feet over the waves in between a pair of rocky headlands.

Patty hadn't offered him back the controls and he'd been content to be their electronic lookout. Now it was starting to itch at him.

Not a damn thing wrong with how she's flying, Mick. So let her do her thing. The problem was that there wasn't much wrong with her at all that he could see. He had her up on a kind of pedestal at the moment and knew it, but he wasn't finding any easy way to knock her back off it either.

"Looks a hell of a lot like everyplace else we've been in the last few days."

Mick blinked to refocus his vision beyond his visor rather than onto the images and overlaid tactical display projected on the inside. He didn't see a thing…

Right. Middle of the night here versus on Attu or in Anchorage. They all were invisible in the darkness.

The flight had been eerily uneventful. No submarines lurking just awash on the ocean's surface. No coastal patrols. Not even any wandering fisherman working the edge of the continental shelf on the bitter October night.

The report of *Leeloo's* safe return to Eareckson Air Station only to discover a failed valve, and *Beatrix* catching back up with them a half hour from the Russian coast had been the only excitement. The tanker that had accompanied the *Beatrix* had cut and run, they didn't dare climb high enough to top off the *Carrie-Anne's* tanks this close to the Russian coast.

The three helicopters had purposely come ashore in a stretch of deep wilderness well clear of roads or habitation. The coast here was a mix of stark wilderness, abandoned fishing villages, and several defunct military bases. Satellite imagery said they had their choice of the last. Commander Altman had selected a particularly isolated former submarine base. It was defunct and stripped. Even with night vision, it was easy to see the wreckage of the abandonment.

Utilitarian two-story buildings, in depressingly blockish Russian style, were scattered about the narrow valley looking more like a child's spilled toys than a military operation. As they flew deeper into the cove, they had to veer to avoid a submarine's conning tower.

It gave Mick a jolt until he realized that the angle was wrong. It was an abandoned sub, run up on a sandbar, and tilted over at a crazed angle. If it was daylight, he'd bet it was covered in rust and bird poop, but there were some details that nighttime light amplification equipment simply didn't reveal.

Their night-vision gear did reveal the many missing windows in the sides of the buildings. Either a departing slash of vandalism by the workers and soldiers who had spent years confined on these desolate shores, or a raging typhoon. Perhaps both.

The overgrown grounds were scattered with heavy machinery, decaying trucks, and old submarine engines. The detritus of a small military population abruptly vacated stretched far and wide. There was no Congressional oversight committee which defined base closures with phased transition calendars. Here, someone had said "Get out. Now! Last boat leaves in an hour." And they had gotten.

Altman guided them to a small airfield, that and the inlet with its rotting dock were the only two accesses to the old base. No roads crossed the volcanic fields and rugged ridges to this remote location. Along the edge of the airfield there was a line of rusted out hangars that must have been used for protecting any visiting transport aircraft from the ice and snow.

There was no snow on the ground at sea level, yet. But it was the start of October in Kamchatka and he'd wager it would be here soon.

He just hoped that he and Patty were gone before it arrived. He'd had enough of ice and snow for a while.

They made short work of the hangar doors. They were jammed partway open, but a haul line attached to the Chinook and a good sharp yank ripped them off the building. Danielle dragged them off to one side before landing her big twin-rotor aircraft.

Their three helicopters and the very sad remains of an Antonov An-26 twin-prop transport plane filled the hangar. They would now be invisible to any casual flyover. Safely out of sight, their next priority was refueling the helos from the fuel bladder in the back of the *Carrie-Anne.* It took a hundred and twenty-five gallons out of the four thousand available for the *Linda* and made Mick feel much calmer. After they topped up the other two birds—which drank half of the remaining fuel at a gulp—they were ready to depart for a return flight to Attu on three minutes notice if they had to.

For a moment, he stood outside the hangar and looked up.

It was midnight and the stars were burning brightly in a pitch black sky. With the nearest man-made light at least a hundred miles away, the Milky Way was a sparkling white streak across the sky like Mick had never seen. A fishing boat always had running lights and a helicopter always returned to base at night—if they were overseas in a war zone it was a very brightly lit base for security reasons. Even camping out had a campfire, here they didn't dare to light one.

Patty slid up beside him. He knew it was her just from her footsteps rustling against the dry grass punching up through the pavement.

"Hey, Gloucester." Mick reached out an arm and Patty leaned in against him. "Here. I stole this for you." He pulled the orange-and-gold knit hat with ear flaps and a pom-pom out of his pocket and tugged it down over her head.

"You stole from the PJs?" Patty sounded both terribly pleased and a bit horrified.

"No, just from the quartermaster. And I might have asked rather than stolen it."

"That was really sweet of you, Mick. Are you sure you're the Mick Quinn I've been flying with all this time? Considerate? Thoughtful? Sexy? Doesn't sound like you, does it?"

Mick had always thought sexy is what women were, not men. Like beautiful versus handsome. Before she could continue her rolling dialog he kissed her on a fuzzy temple and whispered, "Look up."

"Whoa!" Patty's voice was soft and he could feel her head tracking skyward until the back of it rested against his shoulder and the pom-pom stuck in his ear.

At least there was something in this universe that could silence Patty O'Donoghue's words.

"Man oh man, if you ever wanted a lesson in how insignificant all our little worries are. Damn!"

Okay, not so much with the robbed-of-speech. In the dark, bundled up like two Michelin tire people, he leaned in to take advantage of her head on his shoulder.

The kiss she offered was sweetly tender, but it didn't stay that way for long. Patty attacked him as if they were lying together naked rather than exposed only from chin to forehead. A hand reached back to grab his butt and squeeze hard.

With the arm around her shoulders, he kept her turned sideways to him so that he could slip his other hand down her front. And even though he couldn't feel her shape through all the layers, he could certainly recall how her breasts felt as he stroked his gloved hand over them.

Her own hand, the one not still clamped on his butt, had been on his chest. Now it was moving downward and in a moment they were going to be having sex while fully clothed in the middle of a defunct Russian military base.

Mick tested the thought and decided that he was okay with that.

Patty must have agreed, because her breast was pressing against his hand as hard as she was pressing into their kiss.

"Ahem…"

They both froze at the sound of a woman clearing her throat from less than ten feet away.

"Perhaps this is not the appropriate moment," Nikita the DEVGRU SEAL. "But I should inform you that we do have devices called night-vision goggles. Perhaps you have heard of them. They allow us to see quite clearly what is happening, even in deep darkness. Especially when bodies are producing significant heat in relation to their backgrounds. I should also mention that everyone else already has theirs."

"I think," Patty said to him drily, "since that's far and away the most words she's ever spoken at any one time, perhaps we should believe her."

"We could always test that theory," Mick whispered into her ear and began moving his hand again, the one that had been frozen in place halfway between breast and waist.

Patty punched him right in the gut to stop him.

"Cut that out, you two." Napier's voice sounded out of the darkness. He sounded amused rather than pissed, which meant any courts-martial weren't going to happen tonight.

He and Patty let go of each other.

"Meeting time." Nikita handed each of them a set of night-vision goggles and then led them into the back of the even darker hangar.

# # #

The crew was gathered around in a loose circle. Two SEALs, four DAP Hawk crew, five from the Chinook, and Mick and herself.

"Lucky thirteen again," she remarked.

"Absotively!" Mick responded cheerily.

"Hey, that's *my* word."

Napier didn't make a sound that she could tell, but Patty's attention was drawn his way somehow. In the green world of night vision, with an NVG rig covering half his face, he managed to look both stern and disgusted at their interruptions.

"Well, it is, Major," Patty refused to be cowed. "Where do I file a complaint? Made up word. One of. Theft with full knowledge, nefarious intent, and malice aforethought. I'll come up with sundry other charges later." In retrospect, thinking of courts-martial, the last bit she sort of wished she hadn't said.

Napier shifted to face Mick. Patty couldn't read the next expression, but Mick nodded in reply. She'd have to remember to ask later…or maybe she didn't want to know. If Napier had been asking Mick if he was sure that he wanted to be with a lunatic like Patty, and then Mick had confirmed his choice, that meant…

His choice? That sounded way more permanent than a tumble in a tent and a grope on a Russian runway. It was way too close to that "loving him" thought she'd had the other night in what must have been a delusional moment. Nope. Decision made. No way in hell was Patty going to ask either man what they were talking about without actually talking.

Instead, she'd ask Danielle.

But if she didn't like that answer either, then she'd be—not to put too fine a point on it—totally fucked. And then—

"Who here knows fishing boats?" Altman's quiet voice sliced off her thoughts.

"Fishing boats?" Patty blinked in surprise and aimed her NVGs at him.

"I do," Mick spoke up.

"No you don't, Quinn." She turned back to Altman. "He knows crabbing boats. Way not the same thing. *I* know fishing boats—sixth generation Gloucesterman."

"I thought you were a woman. Imagine my surpri—" Mick's voice upticked sharply when she landed her elbow in his gut.

"But I thought we were here to look at drones," she refused to react to Mick's happy chuckle. Next time she'd bait him up and feed him to the sharks.

"Sport fishing. Dad charters out of Key West," Jason "Mozart" Gould, the Chinook's ramp gunner, spoke up.

Patty scoffed at him, but not too hard. She liked Jason. Besides, Patty herself had tagged him for his vague resemblance to Tom Hulce in *Animal House*, who had gone on to play Mozart in *Amadeus.* When she'd explained her reasoning, it had been declared *psychotically convolutional.* But it had stuck and she was pretty proud of that even if he had refused to take up the piano no matter how often she asked him to. Maybe if she asked him to try the harpsichord…

"Next question is who here speaks Russian?" Altman cut back in.

"Russian fishing boats?" Patty said with as much disgust as possible. She didn't speak a damned word of it.

Nikita and Connie raised their hands. And Mick.

"Since when do you speak Russian?"

"Since Uncle Borya jumped ship in Kodiak and married Aunt Verna when I was a little boy. Verna and I learned Russian faster than he learned English, proper *fisheryman* Russian that would have had Mama soaping out my mouth if she'd understood a word. He still has an accent as deep as his hooks *still* reach. That side of the family longlines tuna, so I do know fishing as well."

How much didn't she know about Mick? After two-plus years flying together, he shouldn't be able to surprise her…yet he constantly did. Well, it wasn't right that he knew a language that she didn't.

"That does it. From now on sex is only in Russian until I learn it." Then she looked slowly around the circle.

Everyone was looking right at her.

"Please tell me that I didn't say that out loud." And she desperately hoped that her face didn't grow brighter in infrared with all of the heat rushing to her cheeks.

"You're glowing there, Gloucester."

"Eat tuna guts, Quinn. I've changed my mind; no more sex for you. Ever!" He didn't look worried; Quinn was a smart man. She couldn't wait to jump him and receive her first Russian lesson. Time to bite the bullet. She turned to face Major Napier. A deep breath to calm her nerves.

"Wait! No!" Mick held up his hands to protest as if he could read her mind. Probably could. And the fact that he was probably right didn't stop her.

"Care to explain why you haven't court-martialed us yet? I'm tired of walking on goddamn pins and needles around my commanding officer, sir."

"Gotta admit, Pete," Commander Altman spoke up. "I been wondering the same thing myself. Your unit. I figure you know what you're doing. But I am finding myself a bit curious. Why is it? You can tell by their goofy smiles they've earned it. Didn't take night vision to pick up on what a blind man could see."

"No."

"No?"

"No," Napier repeated calmly. "I'm not willing to explain my reasons. That's an end to it."

Patty opened her mouth, then closed it again. You didn't argue with a commanding officer, even when he wasn't making sense. Especially when he wasn't making sense. Was it some part of West Point training that taught them to play their cards close and confuse the crap out of their people? Based on experience, she'd have to say *yes* to that.

"At first light, you two and Jason will join Altman, Nikita, and Connie on a small fishing expedition. If your boat is stopped, you—" Napier aimed a gloved finger at her chest as if he was going to stab her with it, "—will keep your mouth shut. You will be the idiot girl on the boat who is too mentally deficient to speak."

"Yes, sir," she managed it without sounding too surly.

"First light is in six hours," Napier continued. "I suggest that you spend at least five of it asleep. Dismissed." Then Napier ended the conversation by turning on his heel and walking away.

"Fishing?" Patty turned to Altman because her frustration still needed a target. "You can't fish for drones."

"Oh, but you can." His grin looked positively evil. Of course, being six-foot-four and one of the best warriors in the entire US military made him all the more daunting.

"Humph!" was all she offered him.

"What was that, Chief Warrant?"

"Humph, sir!"

He beamed at her and strode away.

Patty headed over to the *Linda* to fetch her bedroll.

"You feeling okay?" Mick was right at her elbow.

"Sure, why?"

"You didn't keep needling Altman."

"I've got some survival instincts, Quinn."

They lay down pads and sleeping bags side by side on the concrete near the *Linda*. They crawled in fast and still mostly clothed. She pulled the bag over her head until some semblance of warmth accumulated inside; the Russian night was bitter. She wanted to talk to Mick…and she didn't. There was definitely something going on here, and she'd wager it was good, if life would just ease its foot off the old gas pedal long enough for her to catch a breath. After two years in Spec Ops, she knew that wasn't going to happen any time soon.

Her hesitancy came from the same place it did before: the question *what if this was real?*

And the only reason she wasn't tackling it was…cowardice. Patty didn't believe in cowardice. People believed in God or government or that cottage cheese wasn't totally disgusting as a diet food. She believed in facing her problems head on.

She stuck her head out of her sleeping bag. The cold slapped her despite the stolen wool hat. *Damn!* More evidence that Mick was decent and thoughtful. More proof that she really was gone on the man. She was totally charmed and Patty O'Donoghue didn't get charmed by people, especially not by men people.

"You gotta cut that out, Mick. You're spoiling me."

He didn't answer.

"Mick?"

His breathing didn't shift. It was exactly like when she'd been listening to it back in Anchorage two nights ago, unable to sleep next to him despite her exhaustion. He'd been zonked out, leaving her wide awake, because he made her feel so damn…happy.

Shit!

Chapter 10

If this is a typical Russian fishing boat, I feel bad for the Russian fisherymen. Let me tell you, I wouldn't want to go out fisherying in this."

Mick couldn't agree with Patty more. When they'd flown in last night and he'd spotted the craft, he'd assumed it was a wreck left to sink beside the rotten dock when the base was abandoned. Now that he was aboard her, he saw no reason to revise that initial assessment, except that she was actually afloat and showed recent usage. She was sixty feet of sad.

He. Russians called their boats by the male gender.

He was clinker-built, with overlapping boards stuffed with caulk to keep her—him—sealed. Fifty feet long, fifteen wide on the beam, he had a wheelhouse forward and a terribly cluttered main deck.

The crane, winches, and net labeled him as a purse seiner. Which Patty was right about; he'd have a hard time running this rig. The condition labeled the boat as old and very, very tired.

"Boat needs a name. Can't go out on a boat without a name. Terrible luck," Patty declared.

Mick edged down the dock, stepping carefully over several missing boards until he could see the stern. A name had once been painted there, but it had long since peeled away leaving only a suggestion of letters and no hints at all of former glory.

"Call it, Gloucester," he shouted over to where she glared down at the boat.

"I hereby dub thee…" Patty looked up at the sky and he followed where she tracked.

The stars were gone and the air was gray with the dawn and then she turned to the volcano towering above the base. Mount Shiveluch rose eleven thousand feet in a cone of ash-covered snow. A cloud of thick smoke, gray with ash, punched up twice the height of the mountain.

"…*Graynose,*" Patty declared.

"*Graynose?*" No one else got the reference.

But Mick did, "You are so from Gloucester."

"I keep telling everyone that," Patty complained.

Mick didn't bother pointing out that if she didn't protest about being called "Boston" so much, she'd have long ago won the war on what she wanted to be called.

"The *Bluenose,*" Mick explained for everyone else's benefit when it was clear that Patty considered doing so to be beneath her dignity. How the woman thought she could wear dignity and a bright orange hat with a pom-pom he didn't know. "It was the greatest of the Grand Banks fishing sailboats."

"*Graynose* because this is fucking Russia after all and everything is so goddamn gray," Patty just had to get her two cents in about how clever she was. Which was true, so it worked on her rather than coming across as bragging.

There was fuel aboard and several sets of very authentic smelling clothing. Patty pulled hers on with a vague grimace that might have more to do with memories than the current stink.

Altman and Nikita were as expressionless as ever while they dressed. *Get it done and move on.* Jason rolled his eyes and then dragged on the foul gear with a practiced hand. Mick helped Connie into hers, the short brunette clearly knew nothing at all about boats, not even how to wear the gear that went with them. She was a quiet woman who never complained, but was so out of her element here. It was almost like taking poor Sofia up onto Mount Hayes.

"Do you really need to be here?" He turned to Altman. "Does she need to be here?"

"Best mechanic we've got and is fluent in Russian," Altman pointed his finger at her as if Connie was an exhibit on display, not a person. "Cranky old fishing boat—with an engine that I'm promised runs, but who knows how well—that was built and serviced in Russia." He turned back to loading several duffle bags of gear into the boat.

The conversation was done, apparently.

Mick shrugged an apology to Connie. It was hard to tell what her reaction was. No answering shrug of friendly appreciation for his attempt. No flinch at being treated like an asset on a checklist.

Instead, despite being the one least familiar with boats, she moved into the wheelhouse first and through the salt- and grime-smeared windows he could see her inspecting the controls. In moments, the big engine thudded to life and spewed a cloud of black diesel out the smoke stack that stuck up beside the mangy structure. When it didn't settle as it warmed, Connie shut it down and disappeared below. About ten minutes later she returned and restarted the diesel. It had smoothed out and the black cloud shifted to a clear, mostly, plume of heat that merely shimmered the air.

She stepped out of the cramped wheelhouse and onto the deck, glanced at the stack and nodded to herself. Then she faced Altman.

"I left it slightly out of tune. I think that having a truly smooth-running engine on a boat of this age might appear as an anomaly even if there isn't a single thing wrong with Russian heavy engineering. If you want to actually run out the nets and do any fishing to look authentic, I'll need half an hour to rebuild the winch."

"Do it," Altman said and she turned to the task. Altman looked at Mick a little round-eyed. "I'd heard she was good?" He made it a question.

"Scary good," Mick agreed. "If you hang with us more, you'll find out just how good."

"It's an idea." Before Mick could ask what he meant, Altman tipped his head toward Patty. "What about her?"

Mick had been watching Patty move about the boat. She moved without question or hesitation, cleaning things up automatically as she went. Boat hooks slammed into clips. A corner of a net lifted up and practiced eyes scanning its condition before dropping it back to the deck with disgust. All so smoothly that most of it wasn't even conscious. No one could fake that kind of competency.

"This is her space. Let her run with it."

Altman nodded. Mick's word was good enough. Couldn't Altman see how familiar she was with such craft? No, he was a Special Operations SEAL who could drive anything from a diver delivery vehicle—the small subs used by SEALs for underwater infiltration—probably up to a destroyer. But he wasn't a commercial fisherman.

"O'Donoghue," Altman called to her. "Take us out."

"You bet, boss. What would I be called in Russian?"

"*Ya bol' v zadnitse!*"

"*Ya bol'v zadnitse,*" she repeated dutifully, even hitting the accents well. She had a good ear.

Mick tried to stop his laugh, but he couldn't get control of it. Connie and Nikita were smiling but holding their mirth in by studiously inspecting the *Graynose*. Jason didn't speak Russian, so he'd missed the joke.

Which left a very irritated looking Patty glaring right at him.

"What?"

"Never trust a SEAL," Mick pointed at Altman, doing what he could to deflect her attention, but it wasn't working.

"What's so goddamn funny?"

Mick would have to get Altman back for this later; he was enjoying himself far too much.

"Quinn?" Her tone was only the leading edge of an "Irish Patty" threat level.

"Your first lesson in Russian," he tried to dodge one last time.

"Is…?"

No way out. "How to tell someone that you're a pain in the ass."

She huffed out a breath that would have stirred her bangs if she'd had any. "Oh, like that would be a surprise to anyone." Then she turned back to the task of getting underway.

Mick knew he was screwed. Patty wouldn't take it out on a Team 6 SEAL; she'd find her retribution on a much more accessible target, himself.

# # #

Patty showed Mick and Jason how to run a purse seine fishing net. Nikita picked it up quickly as well. Altman was hopeless which made her feel somewhat better. Always nice to find at least one thing Superman couldn't do.

Then they ran their first haul and actually pulled up a load of fish. Most swam free due to poor technique—that she of course razzed them about—but they still pulled up a couple hundred pounds of salmon. She showed them how to slip the bottom wire so that the bottom of the "purse" didn't close and the fish could swim free.

Some fish, being too stupid to live, were caught despite the crew's worst efforts and she had them thrown into one of the hold tanks. Altman had wanted to throw them back overboard. Patty pointed out that being seen having a lousy fishing day wouldn't raise an eyebrow; being seen dumping a catch would attract far too much attention.

Connie ignored the whole operation once she saw how it worked, and continued moving around the boat servicing various systems.

"Careful, Connie," Patty called out to her on another of her passes through the wheelhouse. "You're going to fix the boat so much that the real owner won't know what to do with it."

"This boat is hurting and, worse, it isn't its fault. I can't *not* fix it."

"Makes sense." Patty had taken the wheel as a form of protection, it kept her from doing the cold and ugly scut work of fishing. And it kept her marginally warmer in the semi-enclosed cabin. But she couldn't move around much and the damp cold was really settling in.

She tried to think of something to talk to Connie Davis about to distract herself from the mundane job of "fishing" their way down the coast toward the coordinates Altman had asked for. But she couldn't. Connie spoke so seldom and—

"You have a problem."

"I have about a hundred," Patty sighed and then startled when she realized that for the first time in their acquaintance Connie had initiated the conversation.

"That's the problem. The way to solve them is to address them one at a time. I can't fix the boat, but I can tune an engine, repair a winch, and tighten a linkage. You see it as a fixed boat; I perceive the individual elements of a mechanical system being consecutively refined."

"Meaning that I should stop trying to fight a hundred battles on a dozen fronts and..." Patty reached for it, but could seem to land the thought.

"And fly the route. You are an exceptional Little Bird pilot and an even more exceptional copilot."

"Good enough to make SOAR anyway."

"No!" Connie spoke as vehemently as Patty had ever seen her. "You only see that because you fly with Mick Quinn who is as far above nominal as Trisha and Claudia are in the 5th Battalion D Company. That's three women and one man I've met who are the best Little Bird pilots flying anywhere in the 160th SOAR. Mick Quinn is the one who is able to live up to *our* standards, not the other way around."

Patty felt like the slow child in school who had just been spanked.

"You fly for the 5E," Connie continued in a tone that was passionate by Connie standards. "A SOAR company specifically assembled around our skills—which includes you. A Team 6 SEAL Commander has put you in charge of delivering him where he needs to go. Own it." The last was a command.

"Right. All I have to be is the perfect copilot, gunner, fisher, and mountain climber."

"Don't forget lover."

"Right. And— Hey!" Patty glared at her.

Connie smiled broadly, an unusual event in itself.

"That was tricky."

"I'm a Night Stalker."

With those simple words Connie spoke an absolute truth. Unlike Patty, she hadn't twisted it into a joke with "So sue me" or something similar. From Connie it was a bald statement of fact. And she was right.

Patty had been fighting to be what she already was. What a waste of energy was that!

Then she focused past Connie and watched Mick "The Mighty" Quinn working the nets on a Russian fishing seiner. He'd gotten the others working in an easy rhythm that looked authentic even to her trained eye, except that they weren't catching anything in some of the richest fishing grounds she'd ever seen.

Had she caught something? Mick Quinn had bedded her and collected his manly "prize." But rather than acting as if he'd gotten all he wanted and was now done with her, he was treating her as if he wanted even more.

That worked, because so did she.

"Connie, could you take the helm for a minute?"

"That would be a good idea, especially if we don't want to ram that reef."

Patty twisted around to look back out the front windows. They'd left them grimy and smeared, again because they didn't want the boat to look too clean. Despite that, she'd have been able to see breakers to mark a reef, if there were any to be seen. A look down at the ragged chart that had been left for them showed a broad reef not half a kilometer ahead.

She corrected their course to swing well clear of that. Connie couldn't have seen the chart from where she stood, so how—

"Eidetic memory," Connie explained with a sigh. "I looked at the chart the first time I started the engine."

That explained a lot about the woman's strangeness. Connie could tell you how many times you'd…

And Patty saw the resigned expression on Connie's face. The woman was decidedly odd—the 5E's quiet genius—and it was clear that she now expected Patty to have any of seven different cataloged reactions that Connie was used to getting. So, Patty would do something different.

"Thanks. Guess I'm not the only one who belongs in the 5E. You have the helm. I have a man to go terrorize. I'll be right back."

Connie blinked once, then a second time in slow surprise. Then that smile cracked open again, "Terrorize a couple for me."

"Deal, sister." They traded high fives and Patty strolled out onto the deck.

# # #

"There," Nikita indicated with a nod.

Her observation sent Altman moving into the wheelhouse and retrieving his high power scope. Then he hunkered down behind the gunwale to look out.

Mick followed the sight line, but didn't see anything out of the ordinary. Kamchatka had started out impossibly foreign. Black sand beaches, backed by grasslands and forests turned autumn shades. Like Alaska, the landscape was harsh enough that there wasn't a wide variety of species, but the ones that survived were dramatic. He recognized the dusty, dark green of spruce, the yellow-gold of larch, and the brilliance of white-barked birch.

Beyond them, rising in a jagged line of sentinels, volcano after volcano defined the horizon. These weren't the broad lava domes of Hawaii or the grand old mountains of the Pacific Northwest. Kamchatka bred its volcanoes like a children's drawing: steep, up past a mile tall, with circular calderas at the top. And now, most of them were coated well down their sides with thick snow. The lower limits of the snow lurked only a few hundred feet above sea level. Another few weeks and it would reach right down to the beaches.

Here and there in the jagged chain, one spewed out a long column of white steam. Of the ones he'd seen so far, only Mount Shiveluch, the volcano perched above the abandoned sub base, was violently active. Even here, thirty miles south, its bold head and massive ash plume marked the sky.

They hadn't passed a single other craft in the first two hours of work. In the third hour, they'd passed three, one close enough to exchange a wave. As far as he could tell, the real fishermen hadn't even wasted the energy of lifting a set of binoculars to inspect their craft.

Even in that short amount of time, he'd grown accustomed to the stark scenery. What had Nikita seen that sent Altman into the cabin to pull out a high-power scope? Finally Mick could pick out the faintest glint of white on the shore. Even then, only out of the corner of his eye when they were riding over a wave crest. SEALs were damned impressive to have spotted the tiny anomaly.

Mick's hands were raw and sore from the freezing cold saltwater, but the feeling was an old and familiar friend. A part of him did miss being out on the ocean, though he'd have preferred a better prepared vessel. The *Graynose* had no luxuries such as life preservers or even an emergency radio. They had their own satellite radios and the Chinook was standing by in case they needed a scramble rescue. But the hull was sound and the weather mild. All in all, a beautiful morning to be out fishing.

Though it hurt him every time he slipped the purse wire and let the catch swim free. His fisheryman blood didn't approve.

Fisheryman. Gods but Patty cracked him up.

As if he'd evoked her by just thinking about her, Patty strode out onto the deck. Hands rammed deep into her pockets, she squinted up at the sky, then back at him. She dodged piles of netting and the occasional fish as she worked her way back to him at the stern rail. She stopped a step from him.

"How can a woman so damn beautiful also be so damn cute?" Mick flicked a finger against her pom-pom.

"Thought I was a girl."

"No. The person who I crawled into a double sleeping bag with was a hundred percent woman."

Her brilliant blue eyes inspected him carefully. No poor Russian fisherman would wear mirrored Ray Ban aviator sunglasses, so they'd all agreed to abandon their standard eyewear, even if it meant squinting most of the time. So, he could see her beautiful blue eyes, but he'd wager the squint had nothing to do with the brightness of the day.

"We've got a problem."

"Damn straight. No time for sex, barely enough to talk."

Again, that narrowed inspection.

"What are you thinking, Gloucester?" Did they really *have* a problem and he was missing something.

"That's not the problem."

"Are you going to tell me? Or do I just have to stand here and admire how amazing you look in that hat with a secret Russian drone base spread out behind you?"

"Really? Where?" She spun away from him to look off to starboard.

Mick tipped his head up to look at the sky. The woman was going to drive him mad.

And high above him, he saw a tiny flash of silver, little more than a sun flash.

Mick did his best to casually walk over to Altman with his scope and drag an oily tarp over him.

"What?" His voice was muffled, but he didn't try to shed the covering.

"Company. About five o'clock, very high." Under cover of the tarp, Altman shifted so that only the tip of his scope was visible as he turned it upward.

"Notify Sofia," the tarp called out to him. "Tell her that she has an Orlan-10 medium drone and she needs to stay clear."

"Get the nets back out," Mick moved back to the crew. "You too," he told Patty.

"What the hell, Mick? I—" then she caught his tone. In that moment the puzzled woman was gone and the soldier was in her place. That didn't mean he couldn't tease her anyway.

"I need to get your pretty ass fishing. We've got surveillance. No!" He grabbed her earflaps to keep her head in place. "Do not look up. Fish." He turned her around and shoved her toward the job, hopefully as one man might shove another—he doubted that slim redheads were standard fare on a Kamchatka fishing boat. There was no way to tell if they were under observation or not, but it was better to be safe.

He went to the wheelhouse.

"I've already called her," Connie was tucking away a satellite radio. "I only dared risk a single, encrypted squirt transmission. I didn't want them spotting us if they have a radio frequency package aboard. She reported back that she is staying another three miles above it and the Orlan is only designed to look down. She's loaded with four Hellfire missiles just in case there are any issues."

"Good. Thanks," Mick started to turn back for the deck.

"Are you the Captain?"

He looked back at her. "I guess. As much as anyone."

"Okay. Then do you want to know about the Stenka-class patrol boat that's coming our way, or should I keep that to myself?"

Mick hesitated for a moment, hoping it was more of a joke than it sounded. When Connie didn't offer anything else, he struggled to keep his voice as calm and casual as she did. This was apparently her idea of high humor and he didn't want to spoil it for her.

"Stenka?"

"Two-hundred ton category. Thirty-seven meters long, 1960s vintage. They were passed from their Navy to the Russian Coast Guard. A couple torpedo tubes and a trio of machine guns big enough to make short work of the *Graynose*."

"O-kay." Of course Connie Davis would have all of those details on tap. "Anything else?"

"Sonar says that we're coming up on a rich patch of fish."

The depth-and-fish finder was the only electronic device on the boat that worked, but he didn't care about fish at the moment.

"Can you estimate the crew size?"

"It's designed for a complement of thirty-two to thirty-four, but with the staffing problems the Russian Navy is having, especially in the Pacific fleet, I'd say twenty-six. An awful lot of fish here."

He was not going to ask why twenty-six and not one number up or down. He'd learned not to ask Connie questions like that because she would always tell you why.

He ignored the fish comment, and also Nikita's sniper rifle tucked in a corner of the wheelhouse. One spray from a deck gun and the best sniper in the world couldn't save them.

Back on deck he spotted the patrol boat standing out from shore. It was heading straight for them. He tried to remember. Had they seen another fishing vessel in the area? He didn't think so. The other southbound boat they'd passed had been standing out to sea, apparently to circle wide around this heavily patrolled no-entry zone.

He'd need something to allay their suspicions. He needed…

"Thanks, Connie," he called back toward the wheelhouse. He didn't pause to hear if she replied.

"Get that net out," he shouted. "Way out. Gloucester!"

"Yo!" Patty moved fast.

"Show me that you know what the hell you've been talking about. You have ten minutes to fill that net. I want to be knee-deep in fish in fifteen."

Even before he finished speaking, she had the net spilling overboard in a long slide that looked as liquid as the water it was plunging down into.

"Altman, you keep your ass hidden."

"Some weapons would be handy now," the tarp replied. Gods, he was becoming as unhinged as O'Donoghue.

"Nope. Not a shot! If you're wearing one, make sure it stays hidden."

"One?" The tarp scoffed.

Mick ignored him.

"C'mon, comrades. Get me some fish!" He joined Jason at the rail, watching the purseline wire to make sure it didn't snag as the net continued to run out.

It felt forever and a month before Patty shouted a hold on the net. Nikita eased down the brake on the net spool until it finally stopped spilling overboard.

# # #

Using hand signals, Patty guided Connie in a wide circle back to the leading edge of the net. There she gathered up the lead buoy and with it the other end of the purseline.

Please God, let there be fish here.

She and Nikita dragged it to the pursewinch and hit the winch hard. Thank God Connie had fixed it. She didn't know what Mick's urgency was, but there was no mistaking the tone of command he exercised so rarely. It was a new side of him, captain of the vessel and looked damn good on him.

The winch roared to life dragging the two ends of the wire aboard and pulling together the bottom edges of the net so that this time the fish couldn't sound downward and escape. With a groan from the old ship, the rings came aboard and the purse was closed.

Patty leaned over the gunwale to stare down into the net. *You wanted fish, Quinn, boy-oh-boy did I get you fish.* The net teemed with Pacific salmon, in this season all Coho silvers with some smaller Arctic char mixed in.

The *Graynose* had no vacuum for emptying the net. Brailing up fish in a smaller net was a slow process and Mick sounded like he was in a big hurry.

Was it the Russian drone somewhere overhead? She'd been told not to look up, so she hadn't. But why would a high-flying drone suddenly have him so on edge? That's when she spotted it. On the water, a flash of light caught her attention—a boat. A big one was heading their way. It was the size of factory ship, come to collect their catch.

It was gray, just like everything in Russia. Then she spotted the diagonal stripes of color on the sides—the white, blue, and red of the Russian flag. Russian Coast Guard. Instead of cranes to crossload fish, it had…deck guns.

She didn't know the plan yet, but if Mick said he needed the *Graynose's* deck awash in fish, she'd give it to him.

Instead of dipping the fish out of the big purse with a smaller net, she grabbed a boat hook and snagged the net as far out as she could. "Loop a line there," she yanked it up for Jason.

Mick and Nikita were doing the same thing on the other side.

She met Mick at the main winch with the newly attached lines.

"Let's find out just how good Connie is. This trick can fry a winch that's in factory-new condition, never mind an old workhorse like this one." She slapped the lines in place and hit the winch throttle.

The entire boat groaned under the load as the winch tried to haul the first third of the loaded net aboard.

"Yank the fish out onto the deck, as fast as you can," she shouted.

Mick and the others rushed to the rail and began pulling twenty- and thirty-pound fish aboard by their tails. It was a race to unload the leading edge of the net fast enough that the overloaded net didn't burn out the winch. Her muscles were soon burning from the workout. If they still had salmon like this in the Atlantic maybe she'd still be fishing there. The entire boat was shuddering, but the winch continued working.

Connie idled the boat slowly backward, easing the pressure slightly. A dangerous maneuver that could run the prop right into the net and leave them adrift with a snarled prop and a destroyed net.

Patty almost called her off, then she saw just how big the patrol boat was. It was deceptive. She'd thought it was smaller and closer, but it kept coming until it loomed large on the horizon.

"Russian only now, comrades," Mick called out. "Patty, keep your mouth shut. Connie too. Your accent is Muscovite, something I'd rather not have to explain."

Fine! Though she kept the thought to herself. She was going to learn Russian so fast, that she'd make Comrade Quinn's head spin.

"And don't use the word *comrade* whatever you do."

So much for that. Though since she didn't even know the Russian word for comrade, it wouldn't make any difference. She went on with hauling fish aboard and keeping her mouth shut.

The deck was already a snarl of tangled net and hazardous with a thick slippery layer of fish. They snagged the next section of the net and once again fed it into the winch. It moaned in agony, but it ground the net aboard. They all grabbed and dragged fish out of the net until they had to shake out their arms every now and then just to keep them functioning.

A PA system blared out so loudly in Russian that she almost leapt out of her boots. While she'd been hustling, the patrol boat had pulled up alongside. It was twice the height and three times the length of the *Graynose.*

And it was commanded by an idiot.

Even as she had the thought, a rolling wave slipped under the fishing boat's keel and tipped her steeply over to starboard. Her crane on that side, unused at the moment, scraped a long gash right through the Russian-flag paint colors down to bare metal. Impressively the crane held, but it gave Mick an excuse to start spewing out what Patty could only assume was loads of his Uncle's invective.

She couldn't look away from Mick in that moment, as he stood on a wreck of a fishing boat chewing out the Russian Coast Guard in their own tongue.

It sounded damned sexy and she couldn't wait for her first private lesson.

As she turned back to her work, she wondered what *suka blyad* meant. Mick made it sound very nasty.

# # #

"If you break my crane, you buy me brand new one, you bitch motherfucker!" *Suka blyad* was a fixture of Uncle Borya's vocabulary that Aunt Verna had never been able to purge. Russians used it as casually as Patty O'Donoghue used *shit.*

"What do you mean where's Uri?" Mick hoped that was the guy who had rented the boat to the US military. "Do you see him here? Uri is sick. We are fishing for him. But his gear keeps breaking." Mick kicked the brailing winch and blessed Patty for not using it even though Connie had fixed it, because he definitely needed something to kick.

"Now go away, we're busy." He did his best to ignore the line of men at the ship's railing, eight of them with rifles pointed down at him and his crew.

"You are fishing in a military restricted zone," the PA roared. "This is a closed town. You are not permitted here."

"I am just an honest Russian trying to make a living. I am not some poacher," which he knew was a huge problem throughout Kamchatka. "Now *otva 'li.*" Of course there wasn't a chance that the guy was going to fuck off, but Mick could always hope.

He made a show of looking around the deck and then shouting, "Where's that drunken son-of-a-bitch Luka?"

Nikita hid a snort of laughter poorly and Jason didn't understand. Patty was busy wrestling with a fish that was as big as she was—an out-of-season Chinook monster that had clearly fallen in with the wrong crowd to be swimming with silvers. Patty and the ninety-pound fish made a very cute image, but he'd have to think about cute later…after they'd gotten out of this alive.

Nikita managed to remain deadpan as she pointed toward the rumpled tarp in the corner of the deck. Giving up her boss pretty easily. He'd have to remember to tease Altman about the loyalty of SEALs; again, hopefully later.

He stalked over to the tarp. Along the way he grabbed two-feet of gorgeous silver salmon that had spent its last gasp. He yanked back the tarp exposing Altman curled up as if asleep. The scope he'd been using was stashed under a coil of rope.

Mick slapped Altman's shoulder hard with the salmon, thoroughly enjoying himself. "You useless drunk. Next time, I'm putting you in the net with the stupid fish. Go help."

Altman made a show of staggering to his feet. He mumbled something very guttural about how Mick would rather screw a fish than Patty, grinned wickedly, and shuffled over to help the others drag aboard the thrashing fish.

"You must leave!"

As Mick had hoped, the captain had gotten off the PA and now stood at the rail looking down at him from among his men.

"Yeah, yeah. Once I have my fish on board."

"Now!" The captain shouted loudly enough to not need the PA.

Mick cursed those of his people who had stopped working in order to pay attention to the shouting officer. It let him buy a moment.

The captain didn't look like an idiot, he would know that they couldn't move the boat at the moment without simply cutting the net.

Mick looked sidelong up at the man. His uniform was a working man's outfit, not some Moscow-appointed popinjay—at least so Mick hoped.

He made a show of looking down at the salmon still in his hand, and then as if just thinking of the idea, Mick laid it across his palms and held it out as a peace offering. Then he tossed it upward, flat, so that it paused in the air just within the captain's reach.

For a brief moment of hesitation, almost too long, the captain considered.

Then he reached out and snagged the silver by the tail. He hefted it a few times, then grinned down at Mick.

"*Milen'kiy ryba.*" Nice *little* fish.

Mick looked at the squirming mass on the deck and spotted Patty's monster. At least ninety pounds of brightly-silvered female Chinook.

"Luka, make yourself useful," Mick jabbed a finger toward the fish.

Luke Altman grumbled, retrieved the wrong fish by about eighty pounds, holding up a tiny runt and giving Mick another chance to berate him. At Mick's curse on his father's family, Altman hefted the monster as if it weighed as little as the runt. Mick reminded himself not to ever tangle with the SEAL commander.

One of the patrol boat's crew quickly lowered a line.

Mick cinched it around the fish's tail and it was gone aboard the Russian craft in a moment.

"Now get out of here, *mu'dak!*" The captain walked away from the rail with two seaman carrying his new fish behind him.

"Asshole to you, too," Mick said under his breath. He'd wager that the crew wouldn't get a single taste of the bounty of salmon roe caviar that the Chinook had been carrying with her. He offered a one-finger salute to the captain's back. By the crew's smiles, he'd read the situation right.

The patrol boat moved off, but didn't return to shore, instead waiting within easy range of their deck guns.

Mick spared one glance at the drone base they'd been scouting, still little more than a cluster of white specks in the far distance. They sure weren't going to get any closer by sea.

"Okay people. Let's finish up and get the hell out of here."

# # #

Once more they were all gathered in the back of the cold hangar as dusk rolled over the abandoned submarine base. As she and Mick walked up to the group, she leaned close and whispered.

"Damn, Quinn. You were pretty magnificent out there," Patty made it sound like a tease, but it was absolutely true.

"Careful with those compliments, Gloucester. Might swell up my head." Exactly what she'd figured he say.

"The way you smell, I'm not real worried. But if I ever want a shining knight in stinky, slimy slicks, I've found my man." And she had, which they still hadn't talked about. Now was not the moment, so she chose a different topic.

"Well, that exercise was useful as shit," she addressed Altman as they arrived at the gathered group and sat in the circle of recovered chairs. "And now we all smell like fish. I stink so bad I can't even make jokes about how Stenka-class patrol boats stink." Patty tried not to think about it. It had been most of a decade since she'd wallowed in such a stench.

They'd tossed every fish they could into the hold's tanks. That one catch had taken two hours to load aboard and stow under the Stenka's watchful eye. Whoever Uri was, he'd just gotten a hell of a bonus at no charge.

"And the nearest goddamn shower is in Anchorage."

"I'm sure," Commander Altman spoke up, "there'd be some Russian sailors glad to soap your back if you want to turn yourself in."

"Only person I'm interested in having do that stinks worse than I do." Patty imagined Mick, soap, and a hot shower. That was a hell of a nice thought as she suppressed another shiver brought on by the plummeting temperature.

Mick shrugged. "Ocean is only about a hundred yards that way. Always glad to scrub any part of you, O'Donoghue."

"That ocean is like a billionth of a degree above freezing solid. You're psycho, Quinn."

He didn't deny the charge as he turned to Altman. "So, was all this worth the trip down the coast?"

"Absolutely! We confirmed the location of the drone base and that sea access was unlikely to be successful. Their active response verifies the importance of this location."

"I still smell like a fish," Patty protested.

"Fish are quieter," Napier observed drily.

"So…what? Am I as ugly as a salmon too?"

Napier opened his mouth, then closed it to look at his wife when she rested a hand on his arm.

"This is not an argument you will not win, *n'est-ce pas?*"

It was a pity that Danielle was so nice; Patty could really get into tangling with someone at the moment.

"While we were busy fishing, Sofia was not idle," Nikita shifted the conversation before Patty could decide who to target next. She did notice that after a day on the water with her, Jason was sitting very close to the female SEAL. *Setting your sights on a SEAL warrior? That takes guts. Go Jason.*

If Nikita was aware of Jason's riveted attention, she didn't show it. With her tablet and projector, she was now splashing images against the back of the hangar wall. The scarred and faded concrete made them a little tricky to see.

It took a moment for Patty to get her head wrapped around the image, but once she was oriented to the sea and the white building they'd seen only as a bright spot on the horizon, she could make sense of it.

The Russian drone base was a straightforward affair, not all that different from the sub base the Night Stalkers were now illegal squatters in. Again, a deep cove between protecting headlands, but at the airbase the headlands climbed as high ridges making a long, protected valley. Down the center of the valley was a paved runway surrounded by several small hangars, what appeared to be a machine shop building based on all of the materials stacked outside it, and a set of barracks almost as depressing as the ones here.

At the inlet's shore was a long dock and—

"Is that the stinking Stenka-class patrol boat?"

"Feel better now that you got that out of your system, Gloucester?"

"Much," she nudged her shoulder against Mick's in what she hoped looked like a comradely gesture. How was she supposed to keep her hands off him when contact even through two parkas felt so electric?

Altman rolled his eyes at her. Then he had Nikita lead them on a tour of the base's image.

Beside the Stenka was a smaller supply ship, about half unloaded. She zoomed the image in at various points of interest.

At the machine shop she zoomed in so closely that Patty could see the color of some idiot's hair. "Doesn't he know he needs a hat in this kind of weather?"

"This is still mild for Kamchatka," Connie noted in one of her matter-of-fact tones. "The current temperature is thirty-seven degrees Fahrenheit, though it will fall into the low twenties tonight. Mid-winter here will settle solidly in the tens, with the occasional cold snap down to minus forty."

"Altman," Patty turned to the SEAL commander, "you better get us out of here before it hits minus forty or my ass is going to be frozen to this chair." She could see that she'd hit his teasing limit and decided she'd take her own advice and stop attacking the most dangerous man within several thousand miles. "How the hell did you get this image anyway, sir? Full base view with resolution down to that dude's hair color is just crazy."

"The Avengers were just upgraded with Argus."

Patty looked around the table and saw everyone had the same reaction she did. It took her a moment to find a way to give voice to the sensation.

"I *love* the 5E!"

There were cheers of agreement from everyone. Argus was a concept camera that had survived a few test flights, at least that's all she'd ever heard about it. Someone had deemed it as mission ready and the 5E must be the first team anywhere to get one. The camera was almost two-gigapixels; a hundred times more powerful than the best smartphone camera, backed up by enough electronics that it could shoot streaming video at full resolution. While Nikita's little tablet computer wouldn't be able to keep up with it, it meant that Sofia and Captain Moretti back in the Avenger's control coffin would be able to track any movement they wanted. They could even rewind the video right back to the moment they'd first arrived overhead if they needed to track someone.

Altman completed the tour of the base.

Patty collapsed back into her chair trying to absorb the sheer volume of information.

"What's missing?" Altman asked the group. "Took us a while to figure it out."

Patty studied the image. Nikita had zoomed it back out until it showed the whole base from the Stenka-class patrol boat to…

"Could you zoom back a bit more?"

Altman smiled at her, but it was Mick who spoke up before she could.

"There's no back fence. The runway ends and then there's nothing but wilderness."

"Taiga forest," Altman confirmed. "Miles and miles of open-spaced larch, pine, and birch. It stretches right up into the center of the Kamchatka Peninsula. It is a disorienting, trackless wilderness primarily populated by fox, wolf, and bear."

"Bears," Patty had always thought it would be cool to see a bear some day.

"The Kamchatka brown is only a little bit smaller than the Alaskan grizzly. Making it the third largest bear there is after the polar bear and the grizzly."

Okay, maybe not so much with seeing a bear.

"With the sea so well guarded," Altman continued, "the taiga is also our best route in."

Please, please see no bears.

Chapter 11

You're a lucky bastard, Quinn," Patty commented over the intercom.

"But it makes sense," Mick did his best to offer sympathy as he flew the Little Bird up into the hills behind the submarine base.

"I know it does. But now I know how M&M and Kenny really felt when they had to turn back."

That was true. He'd have hated being in her assigned role on this mission, too. No Night Stalker liked being left behind the action, even in a crucial role.

He stayed low, rarely more than twenty feet above the tips of the trees as he circled all of the way around the massif of the Shiveluch volcano. His night-vision display showed the ash cloud spewing forth from the snow-covered peak as a thick mass. He gave it a wide berth before descending down into the Kamchatka River valley.

They'd stripped the extended-range tanks and the Urgoza missile pod off the *Linda.* The Little Bird now carried only a Yak-B Gatling gun on one side, and a small bench seat on the other. There was no room for them inside the tiny helicopter as the small back seat was filled with the ammo can for the Yak-B. At full dark they had gone aloft with Altman, Nikita, and Connie perched on the seat out in the cold wind. They were facing sideways with their feet dangling down toward the nearby treetops.

At the planning meeting they'd considered fast-roping in from the DAP Hawk or the Chinook, but the roving Russian drone had worried them. Being stealth didn't mean they were invisible.

Stealth tech was properly called LO—Low Observable technology. They were still visible to radar and heat imaging, just much, much less than your average helicopter. And the Little Bird had the smallest signature of any of them.

The *Beatrix* or *Carrie-Anne* would have to remain well back from the Russian's drone base, a twenty or more miles to be safe. The Little Bird was designed for stealthy in- and ex-filtration; they could deliver the team within just a few miles of the target with no one the wiser.

"But why you?" Patty's voice was as worried as he'd ever heard from her. "You're a fucking helicopter pilot, not a SEAL."

Then it hit him, she wasn't whining about the mission at all. She was afraid for his sake, not her own.

"Oh sweetheart," Mick was glad they were the only two on the intercom. He wished he could just wrap Patty in his arms and hold on to her. He *knew* he was in over his head, but…"My Russian is the best and most authentic to the region. I'm the team's best protection if we get stopped."

# # #

Patty knew he was right, but that didn't make it any easier to swallow. Of course he had to go. They needed someone to stay with the helicopter anyway, but—

If only she knew Russian, then—

But she didn't and they actually needed her here. As a Night Stalker Little Bird pilot, she was used to waiting, that's what pilots did. They didn't go walking into a foreign military base with a couple of Team 6 SEALs. The risk factors were off the charts, even if the choice made sense.

At least she was out here at the leading edge. The others were stuck back at the sub base—loaded up and ready to race to the rescue if all hell broke loose. But they were over twenty minutes away at top speed.

Even though they'd all agreed it was the best disposition of assets, Patty couldn't stop worrying at it like a sore tooth.

At least she could keep the rest of her fears to herself. Mick was flying them through intense terrain and needed to focus. *Business,* she told herself. *Keep it strictly business.*

"You've got to swing west here," she told him. "The small fishing town of Klyuchi on the Kamchatka River is due south of us."

Like an artist with a brush, Mick swirled them aside until they had passed a well upstream of the small town. A small town that also hosted the Klyuchi air base. During the Cold War it had been filled with Russian interceptor jets. Sofia's imaging showed that it was now mainly transport aircraft, but there were a pair of attack helicopters that they really didn't want to disturb. The ground here in the central valley was already white with snow.

Turning south and east, they climbed again into the rough ridge-and-valley country of the coast. Patty fed Mick information, trying to anticipate his needs moment to moment. There was a palpable silence when Mick was using all of his concentration. She'd come to recognize and respect that.

"Vertical descent of the next ridge, watch for downdrafts based on prevailing winds."

"Next fork in the valley, swing south. The opening to the north is a false lead."

It had taken her a while to learn what he needed and with how much lead time, but she had it now. The give and take simply flowed effortlessly between them in some high state of synchronicity that Patty had never found with any other flier. And even though they'd still only had the one shot at sex—which had been truly great—the fact that it had the same feel as this moment didn't elude her. She and Mick simply... worked together.

She guided him through a snow-coated saddle between a pair of dormant volcanoes—"Updrafts on the other side here"—and then Mick descended sharply. He kept so low that the nearby treetops were often higher than they were.

"Coming up in five hundred meters on bearing one-three-five," Patty called out. Then she set a flashing beacon on the terrain map to project on the inside of his visor.

This was the final reason that had tipped the mission in the Little Bird's favor. On the Avenger's Argus-camera images, Patty herself had spotted a tiny clearing, not more than ten feet larger than the *Linda's* rotors. She'd have cursed herself, except that it was perfect. A deep hole in the trees meant they could park the Little Bird close to the base yet it would be invisible to anything except a direct overflight. And even then, the black, stealth aircraft would be very hard to spot.

Mick shut down the helo, pulled his helmet off, and rested it on the top of the cyclic control.

Then he popped his harness and grabbed her.

Mick's kiss slammed into her system and all she could do was groan beneath the weight of the pleasure and the pressure of his lips. She hung onto his shoulders, their Russian Bizon submachine guns clanking together where they hung across their chests. She wanted to strip off her survival vest and shred the fabric that separated them. To feel Mick against her, skin to skin, she craved it like nothing before in her life.

His own need fired hers but there was no time.

He finally pulled away with a foul curse in Russian.

"You!" His voice was rough as he spoke to her from inches away in the darkness. "You had better be here, *right here,* when

I get back. God damn it, O'Donoghue. God damn it!" And he was gone to join the others.

Patty watched them disappear into the woods, feeling every bit of his frustration right down into her gut.

She'd never wanted to need a man.

But she needed Mick Quinn more than she needed to fly.

Well, if she'd ever wanted proof that the feeling was mutual, Mick "The Mighty" Quinn had just given it to her and how. Her body was still buzzing, her lips stung, and his foul curses—so unlike the Mick she knew—still rung like music in her ears.

Now all she had to do was wait. It was an hour past full darkness. The mission was planned to last three hours. First light wasn't for another nine hours.

"You better be back to me before nine hours, Quinn."

She sat alone in the silent cockpit. Her only company was Mick's helmet which his violent exit had knocked askew. It still perched atop the cyclic control joystick, but now its empty visor appeared to be staring up at her.

"God damn it, Quinn. You better be back right here, too. If I have to fly into that base to save your ass, we're all dead." Not that it would stop her from trying; it was simply a choice of last resort.

Damned Russians couldn't leave well enough alone, could they? Cold War II. It was as if they wanted it.

Fine. Well Mick wasn't the only one who could tell the Russians to *otva 'li.*

She estimated the direction of the Russian base and flipped them the bird.

# # #

Mick had taken the essential survival courses like SERE, but felt like a buffoon in clown feet trying to follow Altman. Altman led, Mick was in second position with Connie close behind. Nikita moved silently at the rear.

He felt naked wearing only cold weather gear, the Russian submachine gun, and a GSh-18 handgun. Night Stalkers were supposed to wear SARVSO survival vests and FN-SCAR combat assault rifles. They were supposed to wear Kevlar helmets not woolen caps. And most of all, they were supposed to be wrapped inside the best helicopters that the United States military could manufacture, not tramping through the wilderness on a near Arctic Russian night.

However, on the plus side, he was with a pair of Team 6 SEALs. In addition to the same weapons he carried, they had yard-and-a-half long SV-98 silenced sniper rifles over their shoulders.

Altman had said the weapons were hopefully for show, not for use. They would be the team's passport into the camp, and would also give them the perfect excuse to wear Russian night-vision gear—which was about ten times heavier than US gear—but a sore neck was far better than being blind.

Once explained, the cover was remarkably simple. No one in Russia has access to the class of weapons they carried except Spetsnaz. The four of them were armed as Russian Special Forces. Of course they would carry no identification on a mission. And of course they would be the only fuckers crazy enough to be walking through the Kamchatka wilderness without even field packs.

When asked about not having any of those, Altman had shrugged. "I thought we might need the weapons. Can't say that I planned on walking in the back door this way."

That made Mick feel so much better…*not!* Oh gods, he was channeling O'Donoghue. Though being with a Team 6 SEAL who was making it up as he went was still probably the best guy there was to be following.

It felt like hours before they saw the first lights of the Russian base even if Mick's watch insisted only forty minutes had passed since he'd kissed the crap out of Patty O'Donoghue.

That had been a serious amount of fun. He could turn that into a major pastime. Not that he had ever gone for the dumb ones, but Patty was far and away the sharpest woman he'd ever been with. And she could make him laugh even when it was ripping his heart open. He'd managed not to turn back to look at her through his night vision until they were well under the trees.

In the NVGs, Mick saw her flip him the bird, telling him that Patty would do far worse than kill him if he came back dead.

Even now she could make him laugh.

"Okay," Altman called his attention. "Walk like we're the roosters of the world. We've just walked across the breadth of Russia and it was easy. Now we just want a hot shower and a random fuck."

"No thanks," Connie said softly. "I'm married."

Mick wasn't sure if he was supposed to laugh. Altman and Nikita's silence said that they didn't know either.

At least not until he heard Connie's own soft laugh. "You guys. Such squares."

And she led the way into the Russian camp.

# # #

Patty kept trying to think of ways to make the time pass, because as far as she could tell her watch had stopped working. Counting to a hundred took less than a minute. Counting to a thousand...she always peeked somewhere in the two hundreds.

The helo was immaculate. She'd long since memorized the operations manual. She considered pulling out her personal smartphone and reading an e-book she had stored on it. Except that would kill her night vision and she wanted to be ready the second they returned.

Of course that wasn't even physically possible yet.

Her laggard watch insisted that, if they were still on schedule, they'd reached the base only twenty-three-and-a-half minutes ago.

Nothing from Sofia who would be watching from above. Of course she wasn't supposed to transmit even a squeak unless there was a problem. Which meant that everything was going fine except for Patty's mental state.

For a while she leaned forward and looked upward, trying to watch the entire starlit sky that was visible from her clearing in the forest. Maybe, just maybe she'd be able to see the Avenger momentarily eclipse a star.

Yeah, right.

At this distance, spotting the fifty-foot aircraft was like trying to spot a dime three hundred yards out in the darkness. While a sniper with a decent scope could hit that dime every time, Patty was more of a fire-a-missile-up-their-ass-from-an-AH-6M-attack-Little-Bird kinda gal.

She was either going to go mad or think about Mick. And if she thought about Mick, she'd go even crazier. Sure, she loved The Mighty Quinn; it wasn't worth arguing that point anymore. The question of what to do about it was far more elusive.

Napier's refusal to answer how married couples were possible in the 5th Battalion E Company only made it all the more unlikely. Traditional military practice said that there were two avenues. One or the other of the couple could resign and go civilian before they were caught. The other option was going dual military. The MACP—Married Army Couples Program—worked fine for general troops, those who spent most of their time cooling their heels and doing training at some base or other. Even if deployed, they were rarely both deployed at once and never to the same action.

The 160th SOAR was not general troops and a couple either served in the same unit…or never saw each other. And serving in the same unit meant being deployed together and no unit did that. Except the 5D and the 5E.

If somehow she and Mick could—

"Whoa!" Her shout of surprise slapped back at her inside the Little Bird. "Hold on there! How in hell did the M word slip past your guard, O'Donoghue?"

Marriage had been no part of her early life's plan. Someday, sure. When she wanted a good man to keep her bed warm in her dotage.

"Patty O'Donoghue's boy toy now open for applications," she wanted to giggle at the old line, but it sounded more like a strangled choke.

Suddenly the M word was square in her sights and she was getting the clean tone of a missile lock.

"No way. Get out of the kill zone!"

But her attempts to wave the mere concept of marriage aside merely emphasized that she was sitting alone in the Russian wilderness talking to herself.

Which led her right back to her original premise, Mick was trying to make her insane.

And it was working.

# # #

The only guard the team met was at the personnel entrance to the main hangar. He looked lonely and cold, and apologized for raising his rifle the very first moment he got a good look at their equipment.

Full points to the Team 6 SEAL, Mick thought. Altman had it figured. They were obviously Spetsnaz and that was scaring the shit out of the poor guard.

Now it was his job, with his Uncle's Kamchatka fishing trawler accent, to close the deal.

"Just doing your duty, *Starik!*" Mick clapped him on the shoulder. It meant *Old Man,* about the closest Russians had to *Buddy. Tovarishch* wasn't even used by old communists anymore. The youth had long since turned *Comrade* into an ironical insult.

Altman fished out a clear bottle, mostly empty. He took a hit off it then handed it over.

"*Spasibo!*" The guard looked infinitely grateful. Being a good man, he took a massive swallow, then passed it around the circle.

Mick didn't need the slight headshake from Altman to not swallow any. He tipped it up, kept his tongue over the mouth, and then pulled it back down and returned it, offering a sharp gasp as if the alcohol burned his throat.

When the guard gestured to offer it to the women, Mick just pushed it back toward the man. "We have other ways of keeping our women warm, *Tovarishch*." He gave the final word a full, ironical twist. The guard was young enough to have been trained by members of the Soviet Union who would have taken great pleasure in disciplining anyone of the new Russia.

The guard laughed and smiled, then slipped to the ground. Altman and Nikita caught him on the way down. Altman took back the bottle and stoppered it.

"Falling asleep on duty will get him latrine duty. Doing so while supposedly drunk will get him far worse," Altman explained as he pocketed the bottle.

There was no keypad on the door, just a simple lock. Nikita knelt and pulled out some picks. Ten seconds later they were inside and confirming the lack of alarms.

"Feeling too safe out here in the wilderness, Comrades," Mick whispered quietly.

Thirty seconds later, they had confirmed that they were the only ones in the vast building.

As they'd spotted from the fishing boat, there was an Orlan-10 drone parked close by the main doors. With another positioned close behind it.

The rest of the hangar was taken up by four very nasty looking aircraft in various stages of assembly. A complete one stood on its wheels close by the door.

"Skad UCAVs," Connie confirmed and moved toward the partial aircraft as if in a dream.

"Pictures, Mick. Every angle and a video of each one."

Mick pulled out a low-light camera and went to work.

"Software," Connie said, shaking herself awake. "That is the key to aircraft now. We need the software."

"Here," Nikita moved unerringly toward one particular station. It took Mick a moment to figure out why; it was the only one that was a complete mess. She flipped through the papers rapidly, checked under a keyboard and then a mouse pad, then under the mouse. She left it on its back and began typing as she read what was written on the bottom of the mouse.

The screen flashed to life. Nikita plugged memory sticks into external ports.

Mick went back to taking photographs.

A very quiet and intense four minutes later, he couldn't think of another angle to photograph the Skad and moved on to the Orlan-10. He was just wondering whether or not to try pulling the covers on one when a low whistle brought him hustling back.

"Two clean copies," Nikita announced. And yanked out the memory sticks. She handed one to him and he copied all of the pictures onto it. She took it back and gave him the other copy of the software. By now they'd been inside the building for five minutes and had two copies of everything.

While they'd been making the copies, Connie had slid into the programmer's chair.

"Isn't that interesting," she seemed to be talking to herself.

"You know about software as well as mechanics?" Then Mick cursed himself for asking such an extraneous question during a mission.

Connie ignored him as she scrolled blocks of code faster than an air battle shifted tactical screens.

"In modern day…the physical mechanics…"

It was as if his question was slowly jerking a response from her in little dribs and drabs while her main attention was processing the information on the screen.

"…are just a small factor…in performance. The…software now controls…most of the ultimate…capabilities of the…craft."

Six minutes gone and still she was scrolling screens faster than he could focus on them.

Then her voice shifted abruptly.

"I need fifteen minutes," Connie didn't wait for an answer as her fingers flew across the keyboard.

They'd rehearsed this a dozen times back at the sub base. Maximum mission time was to be ten minutes from first contact.

Mick pulled Altman and Nikita aside. "How long is the guard's knockout good for?"

Altman didn't bother checking his watch. "Twenty minutes to groggy, thirty to fully awake and praying to God that we were just a hallucination. If he isn't caught sleeping, he'll never report us to anybody. Sofia observed that last night they changed the guard at 2000 and 2400 hours. It's 2230 right now, so that part of it should work out."

"Do we drag her out?" Nikita asked softly.

Mick was about to nod that they'd have to, but Connie didn't give him a chance.

"Don't," Connie spoke once again in her parsed, jerking way. "Right now I'd be leaving a big digital thumbprint across their software. I need fourteen more minutes." And then she leaned in as if she could meld with the screen.

"I bet we could drop a bomb right now and she wouldn't hear us," Mick tucked the camera and the memory stick back in his parka's pocket and made sure it was sealed in.

No reaction.

For a ten loud heartbeats, Altman frowned at a spot somewhere near Mick's shoulder.

Mick wanted to reach up and feel if it was growing warm under Superman's x-ray vision.

The only sound was the brap of Connie's keyboard, as loud and dangerous sounding in the silent hangar as the chainsaw-burr of an M134 minigun.

"Go!" Altman grabbed Mick's lapel. "You head for the helo. We need to separate these two copies of the data. As soon as she's done we'll either follow or find another route out."

Mick tried to ask what other route, but Altman was already shoving him toward the door.

He was able to stop Altman's strong-arming him right at the threshold to the door only by grabbing the door frame.

"You don't bring Connie back safe, you'll be the one who has to deal with Big John. He's a very protective guy, you know."

Altman slapped him on the arm, "I promise you that if Connie doesn't get out of this alive, neither Nikita nor I will either."

Mick nodded. It was exactly the answer you'd expect from a Team 6 commander.

He ducked through the door, checked that the guard was still passed out, and high-tailed it for the taiga forest.

# # #

Patty had taken to thumping the back of her helmet against the headrest of her pilot's seat. It didn't make her feel any better, but if she counted five between the thumps, it gave her something to do that actually let the watch move forward in time. In slow excruciatingly motion, but forward.

Altman's plan stated that they were forty minutes to base. Another thirty to infiltrate and find the right building. He'd allotted them ten minutes inside and another hour to get back.

By her best estimation she had thirty-eight minutes before it was even time to start worrying, never mind panicking.

One. Two. Three. Four. Five. Thump.

Thirty-seven minutes and fifty-four seconds.

One. Two. Three. Four. Five. Thump.

Thirty-seven minutes and forty-eight seconds.

One. Two. Three. Four. Five.

Thump!

The entire helicopter shuddered with the impact.

Patty opened her eyes, but didn't see anything unusual through the night-vision cameras mounted on the outside of the helicopter.

One. Two. Thr—

Thump!

Something heavy crashed against the front of the helo. Still nothing to see. Whatever it could be, it was closer than the area of the external cameras.

She shoved her visor up.

Nothing but pitch darkness. The starlight that she'd been watching earlier was blocked by a dark shape—one that took up half her view out the windshield.

Again the helicopter shook as if being struck by a large hammer.

Deciding to risk a light, she pulled a flashlight out of her thigh pocket and aimed it out through the helicopter's windscreen. The Little Bird offered exceptional visibility. The windscreen was essentially one piece of curved Plexiglas from the rudder pedals to up behind her head. A small console rose between the two pilot's seats to about chest high, but the view from a Little Bird was spectacular. At least normally.

She couldn't make sense of what the flashlight revealed though. Something thick and brown was pressing against the outside of the windscreen blocking her view all the way up to the level of her eyes.

Then it moved.

A gigantic furry face turned to look at her, blinking in confusion.

Patty tried to think of how to respond, of what she could do. The bear's head was bigger than her entire body and they were looking right at each other from less than two feet apart.

The massive brown bear snorted the air several times—great puffs of hot air that briefly fogged the outside of the windscreen hazing her view of his huge brown eyes.

She could see every wrinkle of his nose as it tried to puzzle out the light's origin.

After a long moment's consideration, the bear must have decided that she wasn't food, or something that needed a good tromping. It looked away and returned to scratching its back against the nose of her helicopter.

Then it ambled off into the darkness. She didn't remember to pull down the visor until the last of its fat butt was disappearing into the trees. And the recorder hadn't been running. No picture to prove her story.

But she couldn't wait to tell Mick anyway.

She hadn't even had time to be scared, hadn't thought to be. Just two vastly different creatures, each in their own habitat, staring at each other across the Plexiglas void.

She looked down to put away her flashlight the moment before something else smacked into the helicopter.

"Goddamn bears!"

She yanked the flashlight back out and shone it out the windscreen.

Mick lay against the windshield.

And his face was covered in blood.

Chapter 12

Someone was cursing at him. A long vivid stream of invective in several languages. Or maybe just cursing at the world in general.

He wanted to curse back, but he couldn't. He didn't have the wind. His side hurt so much from running at his flat-out limit that he couldn't even move. He'd already been moving at a fast jog for a while when he'd been attacked.

He'd sprinted from there.

Then he recognized the voice even though she'd wandered off into Viet or maybe Thai.

"Gloucester," he managed to gasp out. Thank God.

She could curse him all she wanted as long as he'd finally found her.

Patty grabbed his arm and he yelped. He couldn't help himself.

"What the hell, Quinn?"

"Wolf. Bit my arm." He tried to lean down to see if she smelled as wonderful as he'd remembered.

But she spun away before he could.

"Where is it?" She shone a flashlight into the woods. She had her handgun out, ready to kill it. His own personal redheaded action heroine.

"Gone." Really gone. Good and gone. Gone for good.

"You're all bloody."

"Wolf's blood," Mick raised his Bizon 9mm. "I messed up its brain a bit." The submachine gun had been short enough for him to ram it right into the ear of the hellhound that had surged out of the darkness to latch onto him. He'd only saved his throat by getting his right arm up in time. How strange. *Methods to Survive a Dog Attack* had always struck him as a wasted bit of training for a helicopter pilot and now it had saved his life. Leave it to the Army to cover all the bases, even the ones that looked totally stupid…until they saved your sorry ass.

"You just never know."

"Never know what?" Patty was looking up at him.

"Pretty Patty with the big blue eyes." Even in the vague sidelight of the flashlight's beam, they were brilliant.

" 'You never know what,' Mick? Where are the others?" Once again she spun away just as he was leaning down to sniff her hair. This time he got a good whiff though.

She smelled like fish.

"The others?" The urgency of her tone cut through his wandering thoughts.

"They're coming. Or maybe not." He knew he wasn't making a whole lot of sense so he struggled to focus. "They're going to follow. In fourteen minutes. Maybe more as I ran a lot. Unless they don't."

"And if they don't?" Patty started guiding him toward his seat in the helicopter.

That was a good idea. He didn't want to risk almost shooting his arm off again if there was another wolf.

"And if they don't, Quinn?"

"Altman promised he and Nikita would make sure Connie got out safely."

"How will we know?" She buckled his harness for him. Which was good. The adrenaline was going away and the shakes would follow.

And his right arm was starting to really hurt.

She climbed in the other side and turned the cockpit light on low.

He looked at his coat sleeve again, just as he had after extracting his arm from the dead wolf's mouth. No tooth holes, just an in and out where the bullet had passed through a fold of cloth near his bicep, right after passing through the wolf's brain. He probed a finger through the hole but found no liquid heat of spilled blood and no pain. A clean miss. The thick parka and a quick shooting had saved his arm, but the forearm where the wolf had clamped down really really hurt.

"How—"

"Sofia will call."

"Okay."

And there was pretty Patty again, now sitting beside him in the *Linda* and staring into his face.

"You sure that's not your own blood?"

"I'm sure. Damn, but you're a looker, Pretty Patty. I love Pretty Patty," he'd said it before and he'd say it again. Actually, maybe he hadn't said it out loud before.

"You're a nut, Quinn," she patted him on his shoulder. That didn't hurt.

"That's true," he admitted. "Because I'm nuts about you. Maybe that makes me certifiable."

"That makes two of us certifiable."

And then the shakes slammed into him as the last of the adrenaline slid away and he finally realized just how close he'd come to death.

# # #

Patty was still holding him when the call came in from Sofia.

She didn't know which of them she'd been holding on for. To comfort him as he was slammed time and again by the shakes? Or herself for how glad she was to have him back beside her.

When the worst of it had passed, she didn't ease her hold and he continued to lean into her.

"So close," he whispered. "So close. I'm sorry Patty. I almost broke my promise to get back here. That was all I could think as that wolf tried to kill me. I promised you I'd come back."

"And you did, Mick. You kept your word," as, of course, Mick Quinn would. All of her doubts of the last few hours washed away. She didn't just love Mick Quinn. If they survived this, she was damn well going to marry him and he didn't get a vote in the matter.

"I've been injured before, but never faced death. Not like that. Hot, immediate, and horribly violent," his rough voice tore at her heart.

"It's okay. You made it. It's okay," Patty did her best to reassure them both.

"Who knew death had such stinky breath."

She pulled back enough to look at him again. He'd scared the shit out of her first with the blood and then with the babbling incoherence. That he'd said he loved her somewhere in the middle of that didn't quite count, but it was very promising.

She wanted him to say it again, even in babble. But now, with the adrenaline gone, he'd come back to coherence.

Then the "stinky breath" line.

"Don't I even get a laugh?"

Mick Quinn had just delivered a joke about almost dying and wanted a laugh for his punch line.

And she gave it to him; couldn't help herself. It bordered on the hysterical, but that didn't matter. He was okay. The battered and bloody man looking over at her had those same gorgeous eyes she was used to.

She leaned in to find some not-so bloody spot that she could kiss, when the encrypted radio squawked to life.

"Team of three using alternate evacuation route," Sofia announced. "*Linda* cleared for return to base."

Patty didn't key the mike in response, that wasn't protocol. Instead she powered up and Sofia would know they'd received her message when the *Linda* took off.

Chapter 13

Mick's right arm was horribly tender, every move sent sharp twinges, sometimes down to his fingertips and sometimes up to his shoulder and neck—he'd probably wrenched it but good blocking a hundred pounds of wolf. These twinges were less intense than before. Way better than the moment Patty had grabbed his arm; which was infinitely better than the screaming agony as he'd extracted his arm from the dead wolf's mouth.

He flexed his fingers and wished to God he hadn't. His lame attempt to suppress a sharp hiss of breath was thankfully masked by the high whine of the accelerating turboshaft engine.

So he nestled his right arm in his lap and watched Patty fly.

"You're very smooth."

"Why thank you, Mr. Quinn. Now shut up, I'm busy here."

She'd taken it completely the wrong way. Or maybe not. He remembered the smooth soft heat of her in their joined sleeping bags atop Mount Hayes. Nobody felt that good, not even in late night fantasies. But Patty O'Donoghue did. Someday he'd get a chance to test if that was real or imagined, and it had better be soon.

He let his left hand float on the collective, enjoying the connection from his hand to hers on the linked controls.

Smooth, so very smooth.

And he was utterly exhausted. Too little sleep last night, fishing all day—it was hard work catching nothing all day—and once again it was the middle of the night.

Maybe they'd get to leave Kamchatka tonight. They were barely three hours to Alaska. If they could get even halfway under cover of darkness, they could be back to Anchorage the next day. It all depended on how fast the other team was moving.

Patty swooped the *Linda* through the saddle between the two dormant volcanoes that stood as sentinels over the pass between the drone base and the Kamchatka River valley.

A world of white, lit plenty brightly by the ambient starlight to show up clearly across his visor.

He blinked to shift his focus.

Patty O'Donoghue. She was shorter in her seat than he was, but taller than some pilots. Her flightsuit topped by her survival vest and her gun hid any hint of shape. The blocky helmet covered her flowing hair and the lowered visor hid everything but the tip of her chin.

Yet still he'd know her anywhere. Some part of his brain had cataloged her so completely that he'd instinctively know by the way she handled the controls, by the way she moved, by the way she breathed.

Patty hadn't reacted when he'd said he loved her. He'd also been yammering like a seasick drunk on his first sport fisher.

Mick opened his mouth to tell her, but she'd told him to be quiet so she could concentrate. Busting her concentration during a nap-of-the-Earth flying mission would be a lousy choice, so he kept his peace.

His brain switched on enough that he refocused inside his helmet and began watching the tactical displays.

"Swing wide for Klyuchi," he reminded her.

"Thanks. Welcome back, Quinn." There was enough salt in her tone that he knew he'd spooked her with his wandering responses.

"Glad to be here," he'd leave it at that. So glad to be next to Patty that he could barely stand it.

Past Klyuchi, they climbed out of the Kamchatka River Valley, once again circling wide around Mount Shiveluch. The abandoned sub base lay a eleven miles the other side of the volcano. Almost home.

They crested a long ridge that ran vertically down the side of the mountain. Just as they crossed the pinnacle from west to east, a bright flash burned across his display.

The Little Bird's threat warning screamed with the tone for a missile.

But the missile was heading away from them.

Patty carved a turn to go back the way they'd come.

"Where the hell did that missile come from, Quinn?"

"Working on it."

Ignoring the sharp protest from his arm, he reached out and ran back the recording. It looked as if the missile had materialized in thin air with no point of origin.

Unless…

He ran the tape again. There was a tiny blip of heat signature, far dimmer than the missile's, that followed a different course. Then he recalled the empty space at the far end of the hangar they'd just raided. He hadn't given the spot any thought, but now he knew what was normally parked there, a finished Skad UCAV.

Mick decided that he had to risk the radio.

"Sofia. They're test firing a drone in our vicinity. Find it."

"One moment. I was watching the *Beatrix* pick up the rest of the team offshore from a small skiff. They're safe aboard."

"Get away from this thing," he growled at Patty.

"Glad to. Tell me where the hell it is."

The heat trace had been small, but he should be able to see it now that he knew what to look for.

There was only so much heat masking that could be done on a jet engine's exhaust. It was an issue on all stealth aircraft.

But it wasn't there.

"Come on, Sofia."

If he couldn't see its heat signature that either meant that it was gone or…that it was headed straight for them so that its own fuselage hid the hot exhaust flowing to the enemy's stern.

He flipped on the jamming packages, hoping to block any radio transmissions it might be sending back to base, or from base giving it a firing solution. Especially any images of a nasty little American helicopter flying around in its airspace.

"Climb, Patty. Get above this thing. It sees best looking down."

She climbed the side of Shiveluch. They'd been near the peak and would soon be up in the ash cloud above the caldera.

"Yes, up into the ash cloud. Maybe it will be hot enough to mask our heat signature."

"Attention *Linda,*" Sofia's voice was urgent. "Connie Davis says to evade only. Do not use electronic blocking. Their software is designed to go aggressively autonomous on loss of signal from base."

"Now she tells us."

A heat plume of another missile shown bright, close in front of them.

Patty flicked them aside from the missile.

Mick hit the decoy flares to distract the missile and he fired the Yak-B Gatling onto the point of origin. He managed only brief bursts totaling just a few seconds. In that time nearly two hundred rounds of half-inch Russian bullets hammered into the drone.

The missile followed the bright hot flares that he'd shot out to the sides, but the attack had come from too close. The missile exploded close aboard and shrapnel pounded against their frame with pings and rattles and a few hard bangs.

For an instant, they hovered, stable above the lip of the caldera. To one side were the barren snow-covered slopes of the volcano. To the other, so close Mick was looking right down into it, the great bowl of the rocky caldera spread below them. At its center, a boiling pool of lava was mostly hidden behind great plumes of hot ash cloud. It lit the cloud in a dark, malevolent red.

A massive flash bloomed up from where the drone crashed into the side of the mountain a few hundred feet below them.

"Did we make it?" Patty asked softly.

Mick began flipping through the status readouts when the shockwave hit them. He heard the boom, even over the roar of the Little Bird's engine. The shockwave spun them out over the caldera, tumbling them through a full flip.

A dozen readings that had been rising toward redline bloomed into full alarms.

In cascading failures, hydraulics, oil pressure, even fuel flashed up alarms of red panic.

"Losing lift," Patty reported with the sudden calm that came with being a trained Night Stalker pilot.

"Hydraulics one and two failure," Mick flipped switches. "Backup at fifty percent and falling."

"Have to land."

Mick began searching for a landing spot.

Not going to happen. They were down below the edge of the caldera. The steep sides of the bowl offered no flat spots. The center was glowing with an angry red.

"Prepare to jump," Patty had reached the same conclusion.

A piece of training that never worked in reality. It was beyond last resort, it was suicide. But it was better than riding the helicopter down. There was now no question where it was going to end up.

"Rudders going soft. I'll hold it as long as I can at ten feet."

"Roger that." Mick popped open his harness, unlatched the door—ignoring the slice of pain his arm sent to try and stop him—and grabbed the emergency kit from under his seat.

He wished it was him at the controls, not Patty. That she would be the first to try and jump to safety. But you didn't take control of an aircraft away from the pilot in command during a crisis.

"Fifty feet," he called out, trying to spot a good place, but there weren't any. "Forty."

Mick reached over and hit the release on Patty's harness for her. He had to close his eyes against the anguish slicing up his right arm as he reached over her to unlatch her door. Give him a car's seatbelt and an angry woman tugging on his ears in order to kiss him any day.

"Thirty. Twenty. See you in a sec, Gloucester."

At ten feet up, Mick kicked his door open and jumped into the void.

# # #

Patty blinked to clear the sweat that was pouring down into her face. The moment Mick had opened his door, a wave of hot, sulphurous stench washed into the cabin.

Mick had been right; death had very stinky breath.

She rode the helo another fifty feet downslope to make sure she was clear of Mick's landing zone, skidding on a cushion of blazing hot air.

The *Linda* was just five feet above the harsh rocks and moving too fast, but Patty was out of options unless she wanted to go swimming in a pool of lava.

She wrenched back on the cyclic and yanked up on the collective for all it was worth. The *Linda* cried. Every system alarm roared in panic, but she stalled into a hover.

Patty shoved open the door and jumped. She landed hard, banged her helmet harder, then rolled to get down into a crevice between two boulders as the helicopter crashed around her.

Rotor blades battered against the tops of the rocks. Metal groaned and crunched. Something caught and the tail spun by close over her head.

When she dared peek, she saw the *Linda* shredding herself in the flailing death throes that marked all helicopter crashes. Bits and pieces flew in every direction.

A million pieces no longer flying in formation.

The fuselage flipped and bounced. The engine's whine still roared loudly enough to hurt right through her helmet.

Then it tumbled downslope and plunged into the lava pool right side up.

Most of the rotor blades were broken off, but the stubs still whirled frantically above the surface—hopelessly struggling to still lift the sinking and melting fuselage clear of its doom. Soon only the stubs of the rotors remained spinning above the surface.

A strong hand yanked her out of her crevice.

"Mick!" She tried to hug him, but he was already dragging her upslope. She banged her shin twice before she managed to get her feet with the program. Unable to see where she was going, she shoved at her visor, but it was badly star-cracked and stuck. She pulled off the helmet and heaved it down toward the molten pool. Mick didn't have his either.

"What's the big rush? We made it."

"Fuel and weapons."

Shit! Now she wished she'd kept the helmet. They raced up the steep slope. They'd gone less than a hundred yards with that much more to go when there was a loud *Crump!* from behind them.

Mick shoved her down behind a boulder and huddled over her.

Bits of burning helicopter began pattering down around them.

More than that. Bright bits of lava rained down all around them. A basketball-sized glob landed not more than a yard from her nose. She watched it in fascination. A glowing orb of yellow-orange; she could feel its scorching heat like a hot sunburn on a cold day. It sputtered and spit as it turned dull orange, dark red, and finally began forming threads of blackness as it cooled. It had transformed back into being a rock. Molten rock.

"Quinn. I think we should get out of here. Fast."

More lava rained down, a small piece skidding off her parka sleeve and leaving a cut line where it had melted away the outer material in an instant.

He started to race up the slope.

She cried out even as she saw his misstep. His foot had broken free a rock and sent it tumbling to the side. In moments, he was sliding back down toward her. She dug in her feet and braced for the impact.

He slammed into her, but by leaning forward she was able to stop him. If he'd kept going, he'd have landed close beside the melting *Linda.*

"Follow me," her shout felt small in the vast and lethal caldera. "Step where I step." She grabbed up a four-foot chunk of rotor blade that had been broken off during the crash and used it to poke at unstable looking sections of the slope ahead of her.

She didn't wait for his nod, but moved upslope rapidly, testing each step as Two-ton, the silent PJ, had showed her. As she went, she poked her rotor-probe into the slope ahead just as she had before with the ice axe. That had been ice and rock, this was ash and rock, but the idea carried across well enough.

Patty glanced back and saw that Mick was moving well close behind her. Beyond him lay the last signs of the *Linda*. Even the last stubs of the rotor was gone, just the pattern in the lava of where the five blades had briefly laid on the surface and cooled it slightly.

Then the lava spit again and more globs were lofted skyward.

Patty didn't stick around to watch where they were going to land.

She turned and ran.

# # #

"We can no send any rescue," Sofia told him over the radio. "The flares you make and the explosion of the Russian drone lit up the top of the mountain far around. Helicopters they are coming from Klyuchi Air Base. You must hide."

"Roger that."

At least Patty didn't scoff at him for his lame radio response under these conditions. He expected that they were both just too damn glad to be alive.

Mick looked at the snowy mountainscape below them. They were hiding beneath the lip of a boulder fifty feet below the outside of the caldera. He'd scrubbed his face with snow until Patty said he'd gotten most of the blood off.

"Well, it's just like Mount Hayes," Patty remarked. "Snowy peak. Handsome companion. Squatting in the snow."

"Kamchatka Peninsula. Melted helicopter. No cozy tent. Gobs of molten lava raining from the sky. Russian military coming to kick our butts."

"Okay, not so much the same. So, where do we hide?"

"You're great, you know that, right?"

"I am?" Patty made it sound like innocent surprise.

He wanted to kiss her, but that was a road to complete distraction, so he kept it casual. "Sure. Not another person living that I'd rather crash into a Russian volcano with."

"How about if you include dead people?"

"Them too."

"Okay then. So, where do we hide?"

Mick had managed to hang onto the small emergency pack: water, food, basic medical, and a thermal blanket big enough for one.

Patty still wore her survival vest, which could make roughly the same claims. No gloves except for the thin ones they typically wore while flying. No thermal pants, though they still had their parkas. He could already feel the cold nipping at him and his pulse hadn't had time to slow down yet.

"Got to get off the mountain."

"Shouldn't we be tied together?"

"No rope," he'd already searched through the pack. "Closest we've got is some duct tape."

"Well, I'm not going to risk being separated from you. What do we do, tape our hands together?"

The idea of strolling hand in hand with Patty O'Donoghue down the face of Mount Shiveluch had its points. As did the helos that were probably already warming up their engines at Klyuchi Air Base.

"I feel the need…" he said.

"The need for speed," Patty finished the saying for him. "I feel it too, any bright ideas, Quinn?"

He pulled out his thermal blanket. Using the duct tape, he started fashioning it into a long tube, closed at the narrow end and open down the long side.

Patty groaned when she saw what he was doing, pulled out her own foil rescue blanket and lined it inside his own.

Mick took off his coat and taped it to the inside as padding in case they hit any rocks. It wasn't much, but it was the best he had.

When Patty started to shed her coat, he stopped her.

"No, your coat will shield both of us. How are you at tobogganing?"

"Lousy. I always crash into trees. And a big hill in Gloucester is like fifty feet high."

"Well, this one doesn't have any trees, so that shouldn't be an issue."

"Mick, it's ten thousand feet high."

"And we're dead if we stay here."

Patty muttered something under her breath.

"What was that?"

"I said: Before, I was only going to make you go on a roller coaster."

"When we get back, I promise." Then he laid out the foil toboggan and made her sit her butt down in it. He tucked the closed end of the tube over her boots and taped it in place.

Digging around in the pack, he found their one set of night-vision goggles. The visor on the helmets were useless without the information feed from the helicopter, so he'd shed his as dead weight and was glad to see Patty had done the same. He turned on the binoculars and almost yanked them onto Patty's head.

No. She said she was lousy at sledding.

He pulled them on himself and climbed in behind her, pulled himself close so that her back was against his chest.

"Hey!" Patty leaned forward again.

He shifted the Bizon submachine gun from across his chest to over his shoulder, then tried again. God she felt so good leaning back against him. He slid his hands under the harness of her survival vest, but over the parka, and squeezed her breasts just because he wanted to.

"Hey!" Patty didn't sound upset this time.

He pulled his legs in, wrapped them around her waist and hooked them over her thighs. He grabbed Patty's chunk of rotor blade and pushed off. The toboggan began to slide.

Mick locked his legs tightly around her waist so that they wouldn't be separated no matter what happened. If they found a crevasse, well, they'd die together which was probably better than locked in a Russian prison as spies.

As they started to pick up speed, he did his best to watch ahead and steer them, dragging the tip of the rotor blade like a ship's rudder. His arm complained bitterly and he ignored it; there was no longer time for such things.

Her hair fluttered up on the growing wind of their descent and brushed across his face.

To the odor of fish, she'd now added the stench of sulfur.

Charming.

# # #

Patty flew downward through the darkness. The snow spray kicked up into her face. She had to keep shaking her head to clear the snow away because no way was she taking her hands off Mick's thighs.

In moments they were rocketing downward and the wind was a solid roar. Terminal velocity in freefall was a hundred and twenty miles an hour. Terminal velocity tobogganing down a

Russian volcano felt pretty close to that. Tears were being ripped from her squinted eyes. She could feel them freezing along her temples in the wind chill. Unable to see anything anyway, she closed her eyes and hung on.

When Mick leaned to one side, she leaned with him.

When he leaned to the other side, she went that way as well. The snow was deep and powdery. Whenever they slowed too much, she'd raise her feet and the nose of their foil toboggan along with them and once more they'd fly downhill.

It was impossible to talk.

She opened her mouth to shout and so much freezing air and snow pummeled into her lungs that she spent the next thousand feet or so trying to choke it back out.

The ride went on forever.

And for all of it she was lying back against Mick. She was rapidly freezing into a popsicle and it was about the closest she'd ever been to heaven.

"Hang on!" Mick shouted. Then he shifted, wrapping one arm tightly around her waist and clamping the injured one protectively over the top of her head.

She opened her eyes just a second before they ran out of snow.

They hit the ash field going at least fifty.

Mick curled up around her, forcing her to go fetal. They tumbled and rolled down the slope for a long time, finally skidding to a stop in a jumble.

She didn't dare move.

Mick wasn't moving either. The silence was deafening; Mount Hayes had been far noisier.

"You still with us, Quinn?" Her whisper sounded like a shriek.

"I think so. Let me check," he buried his face in her hair and breathed in. "Must be. I like to think that if this was heaven you wouldn't still smell like fish. Maybe this is hell, because you definitely smell like sulfur."

He recovered his parka, though he was shivering so hard that she had to zip it up for him.

Miraculously, he still had the night-vision goggles, so she took them and pulled them on herself. The scouted around and found the chunk of rotor blade back up where Mick had tossed it aside at the snow-ash interface. They had too few resources to be throwing any away. Besides, it would be a very American object, even if it was ten thousand feet below the crash site.

Returning to Mick—who had folded up the foil toboggan and stuffed it in his pack—she took Mick's hand on his good side. They both staggered like drunkards down the last of the ash slope.

They had landed on a ridge of ash between two badly broken glaciers. The crevasses and spikes of either ice field surely would have killed them.

"You done good, Quinn, steering us here."

"Blind luck, I assure you."

She kept scanning upward, but didn't spot any aircraft overhead. Hopefully the Russians were all heading to the drone's crash site now several miles behind them. There was no American wreckage at the site, outside the caldera.

They'd have no reason to search inside the caldera. Even if they did, all except a few tiny scraps had been melted.

If there was enough left of the drone to see the bullet holes or even recover some of the bullets, they'd find nothing but Russian manufacture. They'd be chasing their own tails for ages trying to figure out who shot down twenty million dollars of experimental aircraft.

Provided they didn't capture a pair of lost and wandering American pilots.

She'd finally shifted Mick to following behind. Blind in the darkness, he had a hand locked on the back of her survival vest and was skilled enough that they'd been making okay time.

Still, the stars were fading by the time Patty found what she was looking for.

She guided him up to the face of the glacier.

"It's warm," she watched his profile as he raised his face to the moist air.

Then she led him inside.

Chapter 14

Patty checked in with Sofia who told them to keep out of sight. The slopes of Mount Shiveluch were crawling with Russian military. Hopefully the Russians would give up by nightfall, but during the daylight it would be too dangerous to travel.

She looked around and didn't know if she'd ever want to leave this place.

The ice cave in the bottom of the glacier had been carved by a thermal hot spring. Somewhere up under the ice, volcanic heat and glacier were combining to make a flow of warm, crystal clear water.

The cave was twenty-feet high, wider than her family's living room, and went back fifty or more paces that they could explore walking upright. The ceiling was a broad arch from one side to the other. The surface rippled like pillows.

The base of the cave was mostly boulders, originally caught up in the ice and then freed by the winding stream's warmth. But there were areas where the finer particles had melted out and been gathered into small beaches.

Its best feature was the dawn light. Shining golds and reds glittered at the cave's entrance. The ceiling above, through the thin ice and snow, was a wash of the most brilliant blue she'd ever seen.

"Color of your eyes, Gloucester," Mick said following her gaze upward.

"Twelve hours before first possible rescue. Ready to catch up on your sleep, Quinn?"

His slow smile told her that there wasn't a chance of that.

She nodded back at him, unable to find the words.

"I'll scrub your back if you'll scrub mine," Mick finally said.

"Okay," that sounded fantastic to her. "But you have to wash off your own wolf's blood."

Shy wasn't anywhere in Patty's personal inventory, but neither was bathing naked with a man she loved. At least not yet.

Mick dipped his face into the stream and scrubbed at it until she nodded her approval. The water, she knew, was hot-springs warm, and the ambient air was comfortable enough once back from the cave opening itself.

Still unable to speak, she sat on the small sand beach and watched him undress.

This was not some man barely seen as he snuggled down in a sleeping bag. This was Mick "The Mighty" Quinn shining in the multi-colored ice cave. Broad chest, six-pack abs, and powerful legs. She didn't need him to remove his underwear to know that "The Mighty" wasn't euphemistic.

She watched as he shed that last bit of cloth and then stepped up to her. He took her hands and coaxed her to her feet.

He was so perfect. Even the purpling bruises of the wolf's bite on his forearm—the thick layers had spared him any punctures—only added to the image. How was it possible she was the one he wanted?

His dark eyes studied her and she had to look away from the strength of his desire that shone there. He slowly undressed her, until she too was standing helplessly naked before him.

Patty swayed on her feet, light-headed and dizzy. For once unsure of herself because no man had ever looked at her the way Mick Quinn did.

When he swept her up in his arms, she turned totally girl and just curled up against his chest. He could do anything he wanted to her and she'd be helpless to stop him because she wanted it so badly. From Mick Quinn, everything was welcome. Absolute trust in flight had somehow transformed to absolute trust in his grasp. She tried to think if she'd ever before found such a place of perfect contentment. *Nope. Not once.*

Despite his injury, he carried her as if she were a bride crossing a threshold and she remained curled against his chest as if she'd be there until the end of her days.

Then he let her go and she was falling.

With a splash she landed in a wide pool of the stream's warm water.

"Goddamn it, Quinn!" she shouted as soon as she could stop spitting out the water she'd swallowed.

# # #

If she didn't need to cool off, Mick sure as hell did.

The sight of Patty naked and so damned perfect had been seared into him. He knew he would do anything for her. There were also a lot of things, a whole lot of things he wanted to do to her…or perhaps *with* her.

He'd needed a little distance before he collapsed at her feet and begged her for any morsel she might deign to give.

Even lying back in the stream's water with little more than her snarl showing above the surface, he couldn't stop looking at her. The clarity of the water flowing over her body wasn't helping matters. Her shape was exquisite, a fantastic blend of completely feminine and undoubtedly soldier.

He sat down in the water to at least partially hide the throbbing evidence of his own need for her. Mick grabbed her ankle and yanked it hard enough to pull her face back underwater.

Then while she was still spluttering out her shock, he scooped up a handful of the warm sand and began scrubbing the bottom of her foot. As he worked his way up her body, she soon started a running commentary. First, with each scrub he was a "total meathead." But that soon changed to approval of each thing he was doing.

He couldn't even focus on the words. Instead he simply paid attention to when her sentences grew more and more fragmented, finally shattering under the harsh gasps as she struggled for breath.

When he raised her hips from the water to taste her, her cry echoed about the ice cave.

When at long last he laid her out on their spread clothes and took her, it was his own groans that echoed hers.

# # #

Patty woke in her favorite position, curled in Mick Quinn's arms with her head resting on his shoulder. Her foil emergency blanket was spread over them, but the cave was warm enough that it was all the cover they needed.

The evening light had turned the cave into a shadowed, mysterious place beneath a ceiling of such dark blue that she caught herself wondering why there were no stars in it.

In twelve hours they had spoken no words. Discussed no futures. Made no promises or protestations.

For most of the last twelve hours they had simply enjoyed themselves and each other. She'd never known a man's body as thoroughly as she now knew Mick's, and he was such a responsive lover that she suspected that she'd barely begun to plumb the depths. Something she could easily spend a lifetime exploring.

She slid on top of him.

This time she was going to get her wake-up sex.

With impressive resiliency, Mick's body allowed itself to be teased to life. She cracked open another condom—they'd each been carrying a fair supply which had made them laugh before they'd jumped each other for the third time.

Mick's body shuddered to life as he let out a murmur of pleasure.

She poised herself over him, clutching the foil blanket about her shoulders—when a deep voice sounded in the cave.

"I thought you two might want some rescuing. Am I wrong?"

Patty twisted to glare over her shoulder, accidently ramming a knee into Mick's ribcage, waking him the rest of the way with a harsh grunt.

"Yes, you're totally wrong. Go away, Altman! I'm busy."

"Busy?" Napier said from close behind the SEAL commander. "Looks like you're getting ready to kill the boy. Will you be biting off his head when you are done with him? Like a praying mantis?"

"*Non!* She will not," Danielle spoke up. "Night Stalkers women do not kill their *véritable amour* except with the love of their hearts."

Patty pulled the foil blanket over her head and buried her face in Mick's chest. "True love" was right up there with the M-word as uniquely embarrassing truths to have been spoken aloud by one of her commanders.

"Your ass is out in the wind, Chief Warrant," Altman addressed her. "Right up there with my wife's. Lucky man, Quinn."

"I have to agree with you, Commander. Though I'd say that Danielle's is—" was all Napier got out before Danielle cut him off.

"You! You will avert your eyes and say not one word or I will start comparing you to Lieutenant Quinn *en détail*."

Mick reached his arms around Patty, stroked them down her back, and retucked the foil behind her buns.

"Someday we'll get a break," he whispered into her ear. "I'm willing to keep trying until we do. How about you?"

She nodded against his chest, but was still too embarrassed to face her commanders.

Chapter 15

Thirteen hours flying time saw them back to Anchorage. And Mick had spent most of it asleep in the back of the Chinook. The rest of it he'd spent marveling at finding Patty nestled in his arms each time he woke.

With the early departure of one Little Bird, the demise of the second, and a mid-air refueling courtesy of the US Air Force—because Attu Island was buried in a harsh storm—the heavy rubber fuel bladder in the Chinook's cargo bay was only half-emptied. It made a very comfortable mattress for the return flight.

During the endless hours of debriefing, the investigators—who he was fairly sure were CIA—offered no complaints about he and Patty losing five million dollars of helicopter that would come out of their budget. The intelligence harvest on the Russian drone was huge.

First read was that its capabilities were far less complete than first feared. The airframe existed, but many of the electronics and software packages were little more than frameworks for what would still take the Russians years to develop.

After the round with the CIA, they'd been sent to sit with some engineers as they were the only two pilots who had flown against one or shot it down. Not that there was much to say from an engagement that had lasted under thirty seconds. They seemed quite upset that neither he nor Patty had the foresight to pull the *Linda's* recording log during the crash.

Then…Mick had needed serious therapy once they escaped the debrief teams. He knew exactly where to get it.

Fifteen minutes after they had all made good their escape from JBER, they once again were tucked away in the back room of the Moose's Tooth surrounded by pizza and beer.

Mick made damn sure he was sitting next to Patty O'Donoghue this time. Their chairs were so close together that they were drawing wry smiles from everyone around the table—even M&M and Kenny who were still ticked about missing out on the mission—and Mick didn't give a damn.

"To a successful mission," Altman called out and everyone raised their glasses. "And a safe return." He winked at Mick who winked back.

"Crap!" Patty jolted against him, nearly planting an elbow where she'd placed her knee so solidly in his ribs in the ice cave.

"Our Frisbees. Not only didn't we play a game of Ultimate Frisbee on Russian soil while we had the chance, they were in the back compartment of the *Linda*."

She looked deeply put out by it.

"I'll get you new ones," Mick promised.

"Won't be the same. Those had history," she pouted for display. Then she beamed at him in that way she knew he was defenseless against. "You'll get me tournament quality, glow-in-the-dark ones?"

"Promise," and he sealed it with a kiss. A kiss that Patty heated up until catcalls sounded around the table. Then she sat back abruptly and fluttered her eyelashes at him.

He pulled the orange and red hat, that had somehow survived the mission, down over her eyes.

"To being totally under their thumbs," Napier toasted with a smile. Altman and Big John joined in on that one as the women laughed.

It was hard to imagine a giant like Big John unable to stand up to any whims of Connie Davis…or maybe it wasn't. Mick recalled that no one had tried to argue when Connie had insisted she needed fourteen more minutes.

"What were you doing to their software anyway?"

Connie blushed slightly, not something he'd ever seen before. By the expression on Big John's face that was a new one on him as well.

"They have acceleration sensors aboard their aircraft. They need to track and control the g-forces to make sure they don't overstress the airframe."

"So you switched it off?"

"Seems a little obvious," Patty nudged him. She'd kept her hat down and was pretending she was lost as an excuse to knock a hand repeatedly against his face. He could see a bit of the bright blue of her eyes through the stretched knitting, so he shoved her hat back up on her forehead and she stuck her tongue out at him.

"Far too obvious for my lady," John confirmed. "I'm guessing you set up a failure."

"Not directly," Connie replied. "Too easy to trace. I set it so that when it reached a g-force that was far from critical—one selected each time by a random number generator to make it harder to trace—it would set off a sub-routine in another section of the software. The engine control software would set up a high-frequency and very powerful oscillation that would ultimately shatter the welding compounds that the Russians prefer to use in their airframes."

"Which means the aircraft will test flawlessly on the ground and in simple flight…" Mick was damn impressed.

"But will fall out of the sky under various hard maneuvers," Patty said in wonder. Then she stood up and reached across the table. "High five, girl." Connie reached out and between them (mostly Patty) they managed to knock a pitcher of beer (mostly full) into a Santa's Little Helper meat-red pepper-and-cilantro pizza (thankfully mostly eaten).

"I estimate," Connie concluded, "that will set their program back eighteen to twenty months and add eighty-seven to ninety-two million dollars to their total program cost."

There was a respectful silence around the table.

"I think," Major Napier said softly, "that deserves more than a toast." Then he dug something out of his pocket and grinned wickedly.

He rapped whatever he held twice on the table, hard.

"Coin check!"

People began digging in their pockets.

Mick didn't even bother trying. He hadn't been coin checked in all of his time in the Night Stalkers and had long since stopped carrying the coin from his days at Fort Drum. His commander there had handed out commemorative unit coins so often that they'd become meaningless. To produce one of Goodman's coins was an embarrassment and Mick would rather buy the round of drinks for not having one—for that was the usual price for being unable to produce a unit coin.

At least he wasn't in it alone, only about half of the table managed to produce a coin in the allowed ten seconds after being challenged.

"Let's see 'em," Napier demanded.

Connie and Big John both had coins from the 160th SOAR 5th Battalion D Company. They were beautiful pieces. Inch-and-a-half, die-struck, brass coins. One side had the unofficial Night Stalkers' badge: Pegasus with raised sword and laser-vision eyes. On the obverse face, a Black Hawk helicopter with the regiment motto above—Night Stalkers Don't Quit—and "5D" below.

Altman and Nikita both had coins with the American flag on one side and the SEAL Trident on other side. Six stars had been worked in around "The United States Navy."

"We don't exactly advertise who we are, but the stars are for Team 6."

Made sense.

Other coins were produced from various units they'd each served in.

Napier had been idly tapping his on the table. If there was ever a man who didn't fidget, it was the 5E's commanding officer.

"Let's see yours, Major," Mick called out.

Napier looked down at his hand as if in surprise. "Oh. Mine? Well, it's far better than any of these other ones. Even yours, Luke. Sorry. This one trumps the table." Then he laid it flat on the wood and slid it out toward the middle.

Everyone stood and leaned in to get a better angle on it.

Having the highest ranking coin always won any coin challenge.

It had the Night Stalkers badge on the back, along with the motto.

Then the major reached out and flipped it over.

In the center was a simple large "5E."

Danielle craned her neck to read aloud the words which circled around the edge: "The fine men and women who," she reached out and turned the coin to read the other half of the circle, "make it such an honor to command."

Then Napier picked up the coin, the light brush of brass on the wood table, a huge sound in the silent room. He rose to his feet with a scrape of the chair.

He formally saluted Danielle. "Captain Dellacroix. My honor." Then he shook her hand and handed her the coin.

Mick could feel the tightness clenching in his throat as Napier's wife rose to her feet and returned the salute. "The honor is mine, Major Napier."

Napier dug in his pocket again and moved to Patty.

"Chief Warrant O'Donoghue. My honor." And they traded salutes. Patty was openly crying as she replied and accepted her coin.

"Lieutenant Quinn. My honor."

As Mick saluted then shook his commander's hand. "The honor is mine, Major Napier," almost stuck in his throat. He took his coin and decided it was better than any medal or promotion he'd ever receive.

They each stood in turn and remained standing as he completed his circuit of the table. He also gave a coin to Nikita and Altman who were both obviously touched.

Once again at his own chair, he saluted the room sharply. With a pounding stomp to full attention, they all returned the salute.

"I never wanted the 5E. I already had the best team there was, or so I thought. I was a foolish man. I could never find any better than you people."

With a soft whisper of, "Nor I better than you," Danielle leaned forward and kissed her husband as tears rolled down her cheeks.

# # #

Patty held the 5E unit coin clutched against her chest with both hands. She'd never so belonged anywhere. She'd always been the misfit, doing well, but the misfit nonetheless.

People were sitting down around the table and she knew them and they knew her. She'd flown with them and completed a critical mission, while right in the core of it. She'd saved lives and she'd lived up to the Night Stalkers motto.

"You okay, Gloucester?" Mick was looking up at her.

She looked down at him sitting close beside where she stood.

There was another place she belonged. As close to Mick Quinn as she could get. As copilot, as fellow soldier, as lover, and as…

Patty looked over at Napier.

Conversations were restarting elsewhere around the table.

Major Napier, though holding his wife's hand, was looking directly at her. He offered her the slightest nod.

The major understood the depth and power of that bond. That it could coexist with duty.

She offered back the smallest nod and refocused back on Mick Quinn. She allowed herself a long look into his dark eyes, but there was no question, no hesitation any more. Her love for Mick was as clear inside her as a call to survive against all odds.

"Okay, Quinn. Decision time."

"Fine, what's the question?" As if he didn't know.

She held up her coin, "The 5E. We're stuck with each other now."

"Uh-huh."

"So are you getting on one knee? Or am I?"

Mick grinned at her and rested his coin on cocked thumb, ready to toss it aloft.

The smile that she sent back to him started so deep in her heart, she couldn't have stopped it even if she'd wanted to. Her heart had a hard lock and clear tone on Mick "The Mighty" Quinn. A lifelong lock.

"Call it," he said.

"Heads."

Mick tossed and caught the coin, and didn't show the least chagrin when the "5E" head stared back at him. He knelt before her.

Patty figured they were in this together, so she knelt before him, too, touching her knee to his.

Mick dragged her into his arms and confirmed the target of his own heart's destination with a kiss that sent her blood roaring louder than their cheering teammates.

About the Author

M. L. Buchman has over 40 novels in print. His military romantic suspense books have been named Barnes & Noble and NPR "Top 5 of the Year," nominated for the Reviewer's Choice Award for "Top 10 Romantic Suspense of 2014" by RT Book Reviews, and twice Booklist "Top 10 of the Year" placing two of his titles on their "The 101 Best Romance Novels of the Last 10 Years." In addition to romance, he also writes thrillers, fantasy, and science fiction.

In among his career as a corporate project manager he has: rebuilt and single-handed a fifty-foot sailboat, both flown and jumped out of airplanes, designed and built two houses, and bicycled solo around the world.

He is now making his living as a full-time writer on the Oregon Coast with his beloved wife. He is constantly amazed at what you can do with a degree in Geophysics. You may keep up with his writing by subscribing to his newsletter at www.mlbuchman.com.

Target of the Heart
(excerpt)

—a Night Stalkers 5E Novel—

Major Pete Napier hovered his MH-47G Chinook helicopter ten kilometers outside of Lhasa, Tibet and a mere two inches off the tundra. A mixed action team of Delta Force and The Activity—the slipperiest intel group on the planet—flung themselves aboard.

The additional load sent an infinitesimal shift in the cyclic control in his right hand. The hydraulics to close the rear loading ramp hummed through the entire frame of the massive helicopter. By the time his crew chief could reach forward to slap an "all secure" signal against his shoulder, they were already ten feet up and fifty out. That was enough altitude. He kept the nose down as he clawed for speed in the thin air at eleven thousand feet.

"Totally worth it," one of the D-boys announced as soon as he was on the Chinook's internal intercom.

He'd have to remember to tell that to the two Black Hawks flying guard for him…when they were in a friendly country and could risk a radio transmission. This deep inside China—or rather Chinese-held territory as the CIA's mission-briefing spook had insisted on calling it—radios attracted attention and were only used to avoid imminent death and destruction.

"Great, now I just need to get us out of this alive."

"Do that, Pete. We'd appreciate it."

He wished to hell he had a stealth bird like the one that had gone into bin Laden's compound. But the one that had crashed during that raid had been blown up. Where there was one, there were always two, but the second had gone back into hiding as thoroughly as if it had never existed. He hadn't heard a word about it since.

The Tibetan terrain was amazing, even if all he could see of it was the monochromatic green of night vision. And blackness. The largest city in Tibet lay a mere ten kilometers away and they were flying over barren wilderness. He could crash out here and no one would know for decades unless some yak herder stumbled upon them. Or were yaks in Mongolia? He was a corn-fed, white boy from Colorado, what did he know about Tibet? Most of the countries he'd flown into on black ops missions he'd only seen at night anyway.

While moving very, very fast.

Like now.

The inside of his visor was painted with overlapping readouts. A pre-defined terrain map, the best that modern satellite imaging could build made the first layer. This wasn't some crappy, on-line, look-at-a-picture-of-your-house display. Someone had a pile of dung outside their goat pen? He could see it, tell you how high it was, and probably say if they were pygmy goats or full-size LaManchas by the size of their shit-pellets if he zoomed in.

On top of that were projected the forward-looking infrared camera images. The FLIR imaging gave him a real-time overlay, in case someone had put an addition onto their goat shed since the last satellite pass, or parked their tractor across his intended flight path.

His nervous system was paying autonomic attention to that combined landscape. He also compensated for the thin air at altitude as he instinctively chose when to start his climb over said goat shed or his swerve around it.

It was the third layer, the tactical display that had most of his attention. At least he and the two Black Hawks flying escort on him were finally on the move.

To insert this deep into Tibet, without passing over Bhutan or Nepal, they'd had to add wingtanks on the Black Hawks' hardpoints where he'd much rather have a couple banks of Hellfire missiles. Still, they had 20mm chain guns and the crew chiefs had miniguns which was some comfort.

While the action team was busy infiltrating the capital city and gathering intelligence on the particularly brutal Chinese assistant administrator, he and his crews had been squatting out in the wilderness under a camouflage net designed to make his helo look like just another god-forsaken Himalayan lump of granite.

Command had determined that it was better for the helos to wait on site through the day than risk flying out and back in. He and his crew had stood shifts on guard duty, but none of them had slept. They'd been flying together too long to have any new jokes, so they'd played a lot of cribbage. He'd long ago ruled no gambling on a mission, after a fistfight had broken out about a bluff hand that cost a Marine three hundred and forty-seven dollars. Marines hated losing to Army no matter how many times it happened. They'd had to sit on him for a long time before he calmed down.

Tonight's mission was part of an on-going campaign to discredit the Chinese "presence" in Tibet on the international stage—as if occupying the country the last sixty years didn't count toward ruling, whether invited or not. As usual, there was a crucial vote coming up at the U.N.—that, as usual, the Chinese could be guaranteed to ignore. However, the ever-hopeful CIA was in a hurry to make sure that any damaging information that they could validate was disseminated as thoroughly as possible prior to the vote.

Not his concern.

His concern was, were they going to pass over some Chinese sentry post at their top speed of a hundred and ninety-six miles an hour? The sentries would then call down a couple Shenyang J-16 jet fighters that could hustle along at Mach 2 to fry his sorry ass. He knew there was a pair of them parked at Lhasa along with some older gear that would be just as effective against his three helos.

"Don't suppose you could get a move on, Pete?"

"Eat shit, Nicolai!" He was a good man to have as a copilot. Pete knew he was holding on too tight, and Nicolai knew that a joke was the right way to ease the moment.

He, Nicolai, and the four pilots in the two Black Hawks had a long way to go tonight and he'd never make it if he stayed so tight on the controls that he could barely maneuver. Pete eased off and felt his fingers tingle with the rush of returning blood. They dove down into gorges and followed them as long as they dared. They hugged cliff walls at every opportunity to decrease their radar profile. And they climbed.

That was the true danger—they would be up near the helos' limits when they crossed over the backbone of the Himalayas in their rush for India. The air was so rarefied that they burned fuel at a prodigious rate. Their reserve didn't allow for any extended battles while crossing the border…not for any battle at all really.

# # #

It was pitch dark outside her helicopter when Captain Danielle Delacroix stamped on the left rudder pedal while giving the big Chinook right-directed control on the cyclic. It tipped her most of the way onto her side, but let her continue in a straight line. A Chinook's rotors were sixty feet across—front to back they overlapped to make the spread a hundred feet long. By cross-controlling her bird to tip it, she managed to execute a straight line between two mock pylons only thirty feet apart. They were made of thin cloth so they wouldn't down the helo if you sliced one—she was the only trainee to not have cut one yet.

At her current angle of attack, she took up less than a half-rotor of width, just twenty-four feet. That left her nearly three feet to either side, sufficient as she was moving at under a hundred knots.

The training instructor sitting beside her in the copilot's seat didn't react as she swooped through the training course at Fort Campbell, Kentucky. Only child of a single mother, she was used to providing her own feedback loops, so she didn't expect anything else. Those who expected outside validation rarely survived the SOAR induction testing, never mind the two years of training that followed.

As a loner kid, Danielle had learned that self-motivated congratulations and fun were much easier to come by than external ones. She'd spent innumerable hours deep in her mind as a pre-teen superheroine. At twenty-nine she was well on her way to becoming a real life one, though Helo-girl had never been a character she'd thought of in her youth.

External validation or not, after two years of training with the U.S. Army's 160th Special Operations Aviation Regiment she was ready for some action. At least *she* was convinced that she was. But the trainers of Fort Campbell, Kentucky had not signed off on anyone in her trainee class yet. Nor had they given any hint of when they might.

She ducked ten tons of racing Chinook under a bridge and bounced into a near vertical climb to clear the power line on the far side. Like a ride on the toboggan at Terrassee Dufferin during *Le Carnaval de Québec,* only with five thousand horsepower at her fingertips. Using her Army signing bonus—the first money in her life that was truly hers—to attend *Le Carnaval* had been her one trip back to her birthplace since her mother took them to America when she was ten.

To even apply to SOAR required five years of prior military rotorcraft experience. She had applied after seven years because of a chance encounter—or rather what she'd thought was a chance encounter at the time.

Captain Justin Roberts had been a top Chinook pilot, the one who had convinced her to switch from her beloved Black Hawk and try out the massive twin-rotor craft. One flight and she'd been a goner, begging her commander until he gave in and let her cross over to the new platform. Justin had made the jump from the 10th Mountain Division to the 160th SOAR not long after that.

Then one night she'd been having pizza in Watertown, New York a couple miles off the 10th's base at Fort Drum.

"Danielle?" Justin had greeted her with the surprise of finding a good friend in an unexpected place. Danielle had liked Justin—even if he was a too-tall, too-handsome cowboy and completely knew it. But "good friend" was unusual for Danielle, with anyone, and Justin came close.

"Captain Roberts," as a dry greeting over the top edge of her Suzanne Brockmann novel didn't faze him in the slightest.

"Mind if I join ya?" A question he then answered for himself by sliding into the opposite seat and taking a slice of her pizza. She been thinking of taking the leftovers back to base, but that was now an idle thought.

"Are you enjoying life in SOAR?" she did her best to appear a normal, social human, a skill she'd learned by rote. *Greeting someone you knew after a time apart? Ask a question about them.* "They treating you well?"

"Whoo-ee, you have no idea, Danielle," his voice was smooth as…well, always…so she wouldn't think about it also sounding like a pickup line. He was beautiful, but didn't interest her; the outgoing ones never did.

"Tell me." *Men love to talk about themselves, so let them.*

And he did. But she'd soon forgotten about her novel, and would have forgotten the pizza if he hadn't reminded her to eat.

His stories shifted from intriguing to fascinating. There was a world out there that she'd been only peripherally aware of. The Night Stalkers of the 160th SOAR weren't simply better helicopter pilots, they were the most highly-trained and best-equipped ones on the planet. Their missions were pure razor's edge and black-op dark.

He'd left her with a hundred questions and enough interest to fill out an application to the 160th. Being a decent guy, Justin even paid for the pizza after eating half.

The speed at which she was rushed into testing told her that her meeting with Justin hadn't been by chance and that she owed him more than half a pizza next time they met. She'd asked after him a couple of times since she'd made it past the qualification exams—and the examiners' brutal interviews that had left her questioning her sanity, never mind her ability.

"Justin Roberts is presently deployed, ma'am," was the only response she'd ever gotten.

Now that she was through training—almost, had to be soon, didn't it?—Danielle realized that was probably less of an evasion and more likely to do with the brutal op tempo the Night Stalkers maintained. The SOAR 1st Battalion had just won the coveted Lt. General Ellis D. Parker awards for Outstanding Combat Aviation Battalion *and* Aviation Battalion of the Year. They'd been on deployment every single day of the last year, actually of the last decade-plus since 9/11.

The very first Special Forces boots on the ground in Afghanistan were delivered that October by the Night Stalkers and nothing had slacked off since. Justin might be in the 5th battalion D company, but they were just as heavily assigned as the 1st.

Part of their training had included tours in Afghanistan. But unlike their prior deployments, these were brief, intense, and then they'd be back in the States pushing to integrate their new skills.

SOAR needed her training to end and so did she.

Danielle was ready for the job, in her own, inestimable opinion. But she wasn't going to get there until the trainers signed off that she'd reached fully mission-qualified proficiency.

The Fort Campbell training course was never set up the same from one flight to the next, but it always had a time limit. The time would be short and they didn't tell you what it was. So she drove the Chinook for all it was worth like Regina Jaquess waterskiing her way to U.S. Ski Team Female Athlete of the Year.

The Night Stalkers were a damned secretive lot, and after two years of training, she understood why. With seven years flying for the 10th, she'd thought she was good.

She'd been repeatedly lauded as one of the top pilots at Fort Drum.

The Night Stalkers had offered an education in what it really meant to fly. In the two years of training, she'd flown more hours than in the seven years prior, despite two deployments to Iraq. And spent more time in the classroom than her life-to-date accumulated flight hours.

But she was ready now. It was *très viscérale,* right down in her bones she could feel it. The Chinook was as much a part of her nervous system as breathing.

Too bad they didn't build men the way they built the big Chinooks—especially the MH-47G which were built specifically to SOAR's requirements. The aircraft were steady, trustworthy, and the most immensely powerful helicopters deployed in the U.S. Army—what more could a girl ask for? But finding a superhero man to go with her superhero helicopter was just a fantasy for a lonely teenage girl.

She dove down into a canyon and slid to a hover mere inches over the reservoir inside the thirty-second window laid out on the flight plan.

Danielle resisted a sigh. She was ready for something to happen and to happen soon.

Available now

For more information on this and other titles, please visit www.mlbuchman.com

Other works by this author:

The Night Stalkers

The Night Is Mine
I Own the Dawn
Daniel's Christmas
Wait Until Dark
Frank's Independence Day
Peter's Christmas
Take Over at Midnight
Light Up the Night
Christmas at Steel Beach
Bring On the Dusk
Target of the Heart
Target Lock on Love

Firehawks

Pure Heat
Wildfire at Dawn
Full Blaze
Wildfire at Larch Creek
Wildfire on the Skagit
Hot Point

Delta Force

Target Engaged

Angelo's Hearth

Where Dreams are Born
Where Dreams Reside
Maria's Christmas Table
Where Dreams Unfold
Where Dreams Are Written

Dieties Anonymous

Cookbook from Hell: Reheated
Saviors 101

Thrillers

Swap Out!
One Chef!
Two Chef!

SF/F Titles

Nara
Monk's Maze

CPSIA information can be obtained at www.ICGtesting.com
Printed in the USA
BVOW08s2030091215

429881BV00001BA/104/P